J. (John) Horsley

The Royal Rose

And other Poems

J. (John) Horsley

The Royal Rose
And other Poems

ISBN/EAN: 9783337162931

Printed in Europe, USA, Canada, Australia, Japan

Cover: Foto ©Andreas Hilbeck / pixelio.de

More available books at **www.hansebooks.com**

THE ROYAL ROSE

AND

OTHER POEMS,

BY

J. HORSLEY,

AUTHOR OF "STRAY LEAVES AND OTHER POEMS," "TOUR
THROUGH HOLLAND, GERMANY," &C., &C.

SECOND EDITION.

UNDER ROYAL PATRONAGE.

DARLINGTON:

W. STAIRMAND, PRINTER, 1, HORSE MARKET.

—

1881.

TO MY GRANDSON,

ARTHUR HENRY HORSLEY,

THIS

VOLUME OF POEMS

IS AFFECTIONATELY

DEDICATED.

PREFACE.

THE success which attended my first collection of Poems induces me to issue a second volume, several of these new pieces have appeared in our local and district papers. Some local and historic subjects have been chosen for my poetic pen to illustrate, and may be found of special interest. I therefore venture again to submit my effusions to my numerous friends in Darlington and its surroundings. Though Prophets have not always found honour in their own country, I am willing to believe the local bard may have a better fate.

My love of Poetry has led me to venture my barque on the flood-tide of current literature, and trust that it may find a safe anchorage in many a peaceful harbour.

I have thought proper to dedicate it to my Grandson, Arthur Henry Horsley, with a hope that he may prove a blessing to society as he grows in years.

I have indulged in describing scenes I have visited in other lands, yet it is in my own dear country my humble muse finds a home,—" England with all thy faults I love thee still." This is the country where the pen of the Poet and the pencil of the Painter will furnish themes for the highest intellect and the most exalted genius in coming times as in the years that are gone.

I love to dwell on the place of my birth, and amid scenes where my school-boy-days were spent,— the capital of the Coaly Tyne. Yet my adopted home, where I have made so many friends, and where I have been so long engaged with Literary and Philanthropic organizations, and in which I hope I shall spend the evening of my days, is to me a constant object of love and admiration.

I have lived to see light and knowledge dawn and develope in the metropolis of South Durham, where the first North Country Daily Newspaper saw the light, where the first triumph of Press enterprise— the production of a halfpenny morning journal was achieved—where the Educational privilege of the people outstripped the zeal of our Legislature by pro- viding the Penny Schools, a Ladies' Training College and other Institutions, facilities for popular culture far in advance of the high-water mark of intelligence —to see Darlington rise to the rank of a Municipal and Parliamentary Borough, and to see it face a future full of promise as its past is full of honour and renown.

DARLINGTON, MARCH, 1881.

CONTENTS.

POEMS.

A DARLINGTON TRIBUTE ACKNOWLEDGED BY THE QUEEN.

" Mr. John Horsley, of Northgate, Darlington, known to his townsmen and friends for many long years as a cultivator of the lyre, was induced to forward to Her Majesty the Queen, a reprint copy of the following touching tribute."—*Northern Echo*.

ROYAL SYMPATHY.

The Queen of England lately visited a little church-yard near to Windsor, and after a time of meditation, placed a rose upon the grave of one of her late servants, who lies interred therein.

The Queen of Sheba came with gifts,
    Of costly gems and gold,
And laid them at the feet of one
    Whose wisdom was untold ;
She laid them on the monarch's throne,
    Those precious gifts so rare ;
And listened to the wondrous truth
    Her queenly mind could bear.

B

But England's Queen came with a gift,
　　Where sainted ones repose,
And sweetly, with her queenly hand,
　　She placed a fragrant rose ;
She laid it on the quiet grave,
　　Of him whose feet had moved
In swift obedience to the will
　　Of her, a nation loved.

The Queen of Egypt in her might,
　　With pomp and power and pride,
Call'd purple Rome to see her wealth,
　　And in her strength confide.
And with the lore which Egypt owned,
　　She freely sought and gave,
Till the bold Roman bow'd his head—
　　The mighty and the brave.

But England's Queen, whose sceptre sways,
　　Vast millions of our kind,
Whose power on India's golden plains
　　Her sovereign edicts bind ;
Yet from her mighty empire work,
　　In angel form of light,
She treads among her servants' graves
　　When none but God's in sight.

And, like a sister full of love,
　　Looks on the cold, dark cell ;

She thinks of forms once bright and fair,
  Where now those lone ones dwell ;
Then, with a Christian, queenly hand,
  A heart where love outflows,
She bendeth o'er his moss-clad bed,
  · And leaves on it a rose.

Mr. Horsley received the annexed courteous acknowledgment :—

" From T. M. Biddulph, Priory-place.
" Mr. John Horsley, Darlington.
" Lieut-General Sir T. M. Biddulph has received the commands of Her Majesty the Queen, to acknowledge the receipt of Mr. Horsley's letter of the 8th inst., and to thank him for the verses which he has sent."
Buckingham Palace, 12th October, 1874."

ODE TO DARLINGTON,

As down life's rapid stream we flow,
  And look on scenes we've pass'd,
How dim the distant objects grow
  'Till scarce discerned at last.

'Tis true that visions cross the mind
  Where youthful days were spent,
And pleasing is the thought to find
  Past years fresh charms have lent.

This earth may have its sunny spots
  Where beauties crowd around,
Where Nature hath few darkened blots,
  Where orange groves abound.

The rippling waves may wash the shore
  Where famous cities stand,
And mountains rise where rivers roar
  Throughout their sunny land.

The placid lake with mirror'd face
  Reflecting pictures fair,
Of woodland scenes where pine trees grace
  Those spots of wildness there.

I've stood and look'd on scenes like those
  In foreign lands away,
Where by the Rhine the sweet vine grows,
  And flowers are bright and gay.

But this old town of fame and note—
  The birthplace of railways ;
Whose pioneers such wonders wrought
  In our young boyish days.

I've wandered by the old Grange Hall
  When Sol shone out on high ;
When birds familiar to us all
  On rapid wings flew by.

And when the stars with silver glare
    Peer'd out above the head,
Light-hearted youth the walks would share
    Where shady roadsteads led.

Long ere the forge or blast were seen
    As busy hives of toil,
I've wandered near where meadows green
    Grew o'er the fruitful soil.

Through shady groves to Blackwell Hall,
    By elm and oak and beech,
Where song-birds in their sweetness call
    A good night each to each.

By ancient paths, where Baydale's Wood
    O'erlooks the winding Tees ;
By walks where Carmel blossoms bud,
    'Mid Nun's redolent leas.

From western hills the breeze springs up,
    And sweeps o'er mead and lawn,
Filling with health life's season'd cup,
    As dewdrops after dawn.

Where'er I turn, to east or west,
    Some dear old spot I see ;
Not knowing which to love the best,
    For all seem dear to me.

The grand old Church, with lofty spire,
  Stands out amid them each,—
A watch-tower, where the soul's desire
  A brotherhood may teach.

The dust of generations lie
  Close by its ancient walls,
Who, once with holy love and joy,
  Obeyed the vesper calls.

How often those who now are gone,—
  Whose hearts were light and free,—
Who gazed till every prospect won
  Intenser love for thee.

And glowing youth, in future days,
  When Spring to Autumn bends,
Will wander round those favoured ways,
  Where scenes such pleasure lends.

Where by each walk and wooded lane
  Fair seats of learning rise ;
Where youth in honour hence may gain
  The power to make them wise.

Then ere my days shall shorter be,
  And dimmer shadows come,
I'll cheer my heart with thoughts of thee,
  Thou favoured earthly home.

BY THE RHINE.

Flow on ! O flow on ! thou famed Flemish Rhine,
By fertilized fields of the beautiful vine,
Where, by cities so fair and valleys so green,
Thy deep dashing waters glide swiftly between.

How oft have thy wavelets borne on thy broad breast
The courtiers of monarchs—the loved and caress'd,—
By castle and tower, by mountain and dale,
By dark shadowed woodlands, and lone dreary vale.

With pageant and pomp the lords of the Rhine
Have been merry oft-times with their sparkling wine;
Then hills would resound with their music and song,
As they danced on the lawn with the gay flaunting throng.

Young hearts beating high on their chargers were seen,
The high-minded maidens with pomp like a queen,
While tiller and swain, with the chevalier knight,
Were one in their mirth 'mid those regions so bright.

But castles, once strong, are passing away,
And Time's hand is causing their towers to decay ;
While vassal and chieftain are sleeping close by,
In the silence of death 'neath the dust where they lie.

In days that are gone bold warriors have stood,
With a keen soldier's eye, near the Rhine's rolling flood,
When foes with a spring, like birds on their prey,
Have rush'd on their prizes and carried the day.

The shout from the victors on mountains echo'd,
From valleys below, where the Rhine swiftly flow'd ;
And wounded men lay just ready to die,
While proud victors triumph'd with loud battle cry.

How great are the deeds old Flemings have wrought
With daring and valour, which dearly they bought ;
And that classic land, so noted for fame,
With chronicled pride shall recount their fair name.

True, castles decay in lands of the vine,
Yet the bulwarks of war seem ne'er to decline,
For the strong forts of Coblentz, they stretch out afar
Like high pressur'd valves for the demons of war.

More pleasing the sight are those carvings in stone,
When gliding close by thy cathedral, Cologne ;
Where music's soft tones in sweet melodies blend,
And chorals (not war songs) to Heaven ascend.

Wander on then fair Rhine, by city and town,
Where thy waters have gained such praise and renown ;
Bearing briskly along, as the breeze does the lark,
The full laden ship and the gay gallant barque.

By the low lands of Holland, where Nymegen maids
Look blythsome and fresh as the charms of fair naiads,
Proud royalty reigned there, for centuries long
The pride of Belle Vue, where its princes would throng.

How sweet when the sun in his majesty shines,
With splendour and beauty o'er clustering vines ;
When crimson streaks fade o'er the silver lined cloud,
And dark rolling ones make for them a night shroud.

When orange tints dance on thy sparkling stream,
And the bright stars of night come out like a dream ;
Then thoughts of the mind with force flow along,
And visions of beauty burst forth into song.

Like songs of the Lark, as he soars to the sky
And warbles his notes, as he flutters on high,—
When Spring with its flowers and blossoms are seen,
And earth spreads around its carpet so green.

By thy shores bonny Bingen, I lingered close by
When vine shaded hills have been tinged with gold dye,
When the beams of fair Luna with soft silver light
Dipp'd her beautiful wings in thy streams in the night.

Adieu then, adieu to thy historic shores !
Yet memory shall class them among her rich stores ;
And lands of the Rhine, with scenes so complete,
Shall live in the mind till again we shall meet.

ON WOMAN.

I would ere drops this mortal coil
From earthly care and worldly toil
Sing one sweet loving song of praise
Ere comes the night of my life's days ;

And Woman, thou shalt be the theme,
The noble-minded of man's dream ;
For lo, within her throbbing breast
There beats a heart with love possess'd,
Both pure and good when truth's the way,
But when perturbed, what force can stay,
For since her foot in Eden trod,
And bowed to worship her great God,—
Through all the stream of flowing time
She has with love and truth sublime
Marked out a path of silver light
Like shining stars in ebon night.
How true when her young loving heart
Sends out the keen impassioned dart ;
No hand that holds the polished shield
But to her force of power must yield.
Yet in that heart, so sweet and fair,
There flows a mystic fountain there ;
If grace should from that fountain flow
She'll scatter joys on all below ;
If learning be the guiding power
'Tis like the edge that cuts the flower ;
But if her heart dark bodings hold,
Then woe to those her fashions mould.
She stands alone in conquering skill,
And all must bend to her strong will ;
If mortal cares disturb the breast
She hushes them to quiet rest,

And with her gentle hand sustains
The soul of man, with all his pains.
She stood by Him, who bowed His head,
When Roman guards in wildness fled ;
And in the early morn was seen
With Him, who 'mongst the dead had been.
When her firstborn she fondly viewed,
On it the flowers of love she strewed ;
She kissed its cheeks with tender care,
Then breathed on it a mother's prayer.
When he who had her treasure been—
Through loving life his fairest queen—
When burning fever racked his head
She bathed his brow, and smoothed his bed,
And mourned when he no more could be
Her joy in life's serenity.
Her Maker, in His care and love,
Sent man this angel from above :
And she has been an angel true,
To scatter flowers where briars grew.
The poor, the sick, can never fail
To find some Florence Nightingale,—
Grace Darling, from her island home,
Who braved the ocean's surge and foam,
And brought poor wrecked ones to the shore
With hero heart and pliant oar.
Now, though the world hath ever found
Some moral waste—some barren ground—

With plodding feet and smiling face
She's made it one sweet spot of grace.
Imprisoned ones entranced have stood
To hear the voice of one so good ;
How sweet the whispers of her love,
How calm the thoughts her passions move,
How sweet the charms of her bright face
Where'er on earth she finds a place.
'Tis not her smiles or rosy bloom,
'Tis not her style or dashing plume
That gives to her such vast control,—
It is her mind and gifted soul.

THE EMPTIED SADDLE.

(A MEMOIR OF AFGHANISTAN.)

A trooper rode across the plain
　　Brave and dauntless near his foes,
His fleeting charger toss'd its mane
　　As if to shield him from their blows.

The withered turf rose at its feet,
　　When dashing o'er the sods it flew ;
Its rider had a foe to meet,
　　And ghastly death stood in his view.

He bore a message in his breast,
   Advancing armies to draw nigh,
So o'er the fatal fields he press'd,
   To conquer, or perchance to die.

The deadly missiles of the foe
   Swept swiftly o'er his shieldless head,
Till near the goal where he should go
   He fell among the quiet dead.

The charger found its rider gone,
   Then rush'd towards the camp again ;
Alas ! his object was not won,
   Its rider lay among the slain.

No friend was there to staunch the wound,
   Or listen to his last good-bye ;
No loving maid could there be found
   To grasp the hand so soon to die.

No soothing words came from the lips
   Of one who watched through life his care ;
But there alone death's cup he sips,
   With glory phantomed in the air.

Did he not ask for peace, and pray,
   Though faint his dying lips might move—
While like a soldier brave he lay
   With heaven's clear azure sky above ?

The thoughts of home and friends might press
   Across his struggling, tortured breast,
While transient hopes of life, alas !
   Would vanish into quiet rest.

Now still in death that soldier lay
   'Mid struggling foes and cannon roar,
No more the call to arms obey,
   Or o'er rough Afghan mountains soar.

The bloom of youth his visage bore,
   With eyes as bright as diamonds are ;
His fall (what loving hearts deplore)
   Through blighting blasts of deadly war.

And thus are emptied saddles found,
   Which loved ones fill'd with honour true ;
And hopes which kindly friendship bound
   Have vanished now like morning dew.

ON THE CELEBRATION OF THE RAILWAY JUBILEE,

HELD AT DARLINGTON, SEPTEMBER 27TH, 1875.

See England's sons in mighty phalanx throng,
With banners floating in the breeze so free,
To celebrate with joy, in speech and song,
The triumphs of a Railway Jubilee.

The tribes of Judah once with gladness hail'd
Their Jubilee, in city, hill, and strand ;
While the shrill note of trumpets never fail'd
To echo through their bright and sunny land.

Then slave and serf alike, were truly free,
And timbrels sounded to their merry dance,
Amid the joyful shouts of jubilee,
Such as ne'er was heard in gay, heroic France.

'Tis fifty years since Stephenson and Pease
Stood wondering at the force and power of steam,
Close by the town that skirts the classic Tees,
Seeming to them, like visions in a dream.

Their scheme was small when first it was begun,
Like Art and Science in the early days ;
But, noble-minded, they their task have won,
And now o'er earth it sheds its brightest rays.

But then they dreamt not that a new era
Had dawn'd so bright upon the human race,
When Roman roads would quickly pass away,
And iron rails, instead, should take their place.

And quick as lightning through the murky air
The dashing train would speed its onward course ;
By night or day, in stormy ones, or fair,
Nought should impede its giant force.

E'en Alpine heights, though clothed in garb of snow,
Should soon be scaled in safety and with ease,
As British barques 'mid summer breezes go,
Calmly o'er the deep, unruffled seas,

And now that fifty years have pass'd away,
And lines are laid through Russia's regions cold,
And climes were Sol sends down his burning ray,
Or where Columbus stood amid his crew so bold.—

Who would have dreamt the young, but thinking Watt,
As o'er the fire he watch'd the boiling steam.
Would to the world be more than autocrat,
Though no sparkling gems adorn his diadem?

For steam and railways in the fleeting past
Have chang'd the world and made it wond'rous new;
And Time, as it rolls on, may change at last
E'en these, for science brings strange things to view.

The iron rail will be the great highway
For trade and truth to roll their precious freight
And spots where darkness has the rule and sway
Will change from ignorance and the gloom of night.

For those who know each other but in name
Will soon be join'd in bonds of brotherhood;
And war, with all its deadly brands of flame,
Shall cease, for men to do each other good.

PIONEERS OF THE RAILWAY SYSTEM.

BORN JUNE 9TH 1781, DIED AUGT 12TH 1848.

GEO. STEPHENSON.

BORN MAY 31ST 1767, DIED JULY 31ST 1858.

EDWARD PEASE.

The First Locomotive Engine employed on a Public Railway.

THIS ENGINE WAS BUILT BY GEO. STEPHENSON IN 1825 & CONTINUED TO RUN ON THE STOCKTON & DARLINGTON RAILWAY UNTIL 1850.

BORN JUNE 22ND 1799, DIED FEBY 8TH 1872.

J. PEASE JUNR

BORN NOVR 30TH 1725, DIED JUNE 11TH 186?

FRA. NEWBURN.

Though " Number One " to us looks strange in make,
What changes have been wrought since first it ran !
The engines of to-day in form and shape
Are perfect, through the skill and power of man.

How strange the sight when, on that autumn day,
The wondering multitude beheld it move ;
When from the west it stole so smooth away,
While numbers thought a failure it would prove.

Yet nought on earth hath been so wond'rous great
Since Adam till'd in Paradise the soil ;
Then honour to the men who could create,
And help to ease the labouring sons of toil.

How fitting, too, that on this gladsome day,
To Joseph Pease a Statue should be raised—
To perpetuate a name on Time's railway,
And be by future generations prais'd.

Thanks to Hackworth, Stephenson, and Edward Pease,
To Meynell, Mewburn—men who led the van ;
Who never did despair though trials did increase
But boldly persevered, and carried out their plan.

And hail to those who too have pass'd away,
Who lived and worked with quiet power and will ;
The persevering Dixon, the gentle T. MacNay,
And others famed for engineering skill.

Yea, praise to all who plann'd the railway scheme,
And cycles, as they roll, still the cry shall be,
" Loud praise for Railways, Telegraphs and Steam,
For glorious England, and this Jubilee ! "

NOTE.—During the last fifty years there have been 200,000 miles
of railway laid down throughout the world, of which the
United Kingdom has 16,448 miles ; America, 75,000 ;
Russia, 10,000; Germany, 13,000; France, 11,000 ;
Austria, 10,000 ; and India, 6,000.   The paid-up capital
of the United Kingdom, £609,949,919.   The number of
passengers in 1874 was 478,000,000, and the working
expenses £32,000,000, all of which looks like an Arabian
Night's Tale, springing up from the Darlington and
Stockton Railway since 1825.

HAUGHTON PARISH CHURCH.*

I love those gray old furred walls,
   On which the hand of Time is press'd ;
There, memory to my soul recalls
   Past generations now at rest.

Bright ivy clings around thy tower,
   As if to shield thee from the storm :
To save thee from Time's wreckful power
   And still preserve thy Saxon form.

Within that sacred solemn pile
   Where mouldering oak in carved device
Stands out so bold amid each aisle,
   There shines the pearl of costless price.

* It has been a place of Worship for 800 years.   The Rev. E.
Cheese is Rector.

From thence the vows of many a saint
   Have gone to Heaven's eternal King.
When heart and soul were sick and faint,
   And human aid no strength could bring.

The evening hymn so sweetly sung,
   The evening prayer sincerely given,
Like chords from harps in sweetness strung,
   Have reached the golden gates of Heaven.

There men of God with souls sincere
   Have led their flock to fountains bright :
Have led them where the streams are clear,
   Where Seraphs bask in crystal light.

The village maid with cheeks so fair
   Came here when Sabbath sounds were nigh ;
Then with a sweet and softened prayer
   Looked up for help beyond the sky.

The aged one with trembling limb,
   With feeble knee and faltering voice,
Whose form was bent, whose eyes were dim,
   Met here with loved ones to rejoice.

But these have passed time's lengthened bound,
   The aged saint, the village maid,
No more these walls their notes resound,
   For side by side their dust is laid.

Though generations thus have gone
  To sleep beneath thy moss-clad tower;
Yet generations still press on
  To worship at the evening hour.

O, may the gospel, pure and free,
  Be truly taught within thy walls,
And thousands bend in prayer the knee
  To Jesus, who so sweetly calls.

BURIED WHERE THE SNOW-FLAKES FELL.

Thou art gone, sweet child,
Where all seasons are mild;
  To the far plains of Heaven,
Where the trees of life grow,
And no winter storms blow,
  And no dark clouds are driven.

Thou art gone where the day
Never passes away,
  And the night time's unknown;
Where the angel forms move
In their grace and their love,
  And where life's streams are flowing.

Thou art gone where the tear
Never more shall appear
  On the pale sunken cheek;

But where the white-rob'd throng
Sing their sweet Sabbath song,
    With the just ones and meek.

They have laid thee below
The beautiful snow
    In thy clay-moulded bed;
But though snow-flakes come fast,
And fierce blows the blast,
    They disturb not thy head;

For thy little hands rest
On thy lifeless breast,
    And thy ears hear no sound;
With thine eyeballs enclosed,
As in slumber reposed
    In the cold-vaulted ground.

But thy soul's on the wing,
Far away from death's sting,
    And the darkness below;
Thou art basking in light,
As pure and as white
    As the beautiful snow.

ON THE DARLINGTON FLOWER MISSION.

"Inasmuch as ye have done it unto one of the least of these
My brethren, ye have done it unto Me."

'Tis sweet when summer seasons come,
 'Mid all their sunny hours,
To wander forth, with joy and health,
 Among the fragrant flowers.

The loving God hath sent them here—
 Those gems of earthly bowers ;
O, who can say they do not prize
 The gay, enchanting flowers ?

The forests teem with every hue,
 When freshened with the showers,
That young and old alike may love
 The wild, the woodland flowers.

The rich have many an Eden spread
 Around their stately towers,
Aromas scent their every step
 With essence from the flowers.

And God has sent those lovely things,
 With liberal hand He pours ;
To high and low alike He gives
 The brightest garland flowers.

Now many a mortal lies distressed*
   Doomed to dark and lonely hours,
Who would rejoice could they but look
   On one fair bunch of flowers.

The weary child who, sinking, lies
   Where fever heat devours,
Would smile with joy, could he but grasp
   A gift of blooming flowers.

Go pluck them, gentle lady, then,
   The task is truly yours,
And send to each sick-room a few
   Of your sweet garden flowers.

And He who taught, by lilies fair—
   Those teachings should be ours—
That He will surely care for you
   If He doth care for flowers;

The Rose of Sharon will perfume
   Those noble deeds of yours;
And you shall tread where angels tread,
   'Midst never-fading flowers.

* So overjoyed was one, who had been ill for six months,
that when presented with a bunch of flowers he burst into tears
at the sight of them.

IN MEMORY OF THE LATE MR. CHARLES PEASE,

Who Died July 9th, 1873, Aged 30 Years.

There's sorrow in that silent hall,
    Though all around looks calm and still,
While evening shades in sweetness fall
    So gently on its moss-clad hill.

There, pale and calm within its walls
    In silent death, as if he slept,
Lies one whom memory now recalls
    Past joys that o'er his pathway swept.

O, how we hop'd, as men oft do
    Who dress the young and tender plant,
That autumn might its blessings strew,
    And yield the joys we mortals want.

How fondly did men hope to see
    His manhood full fruition yield ;
But death, which sets all spirits free,
    On his kind heart its impress sealed.

There is no heart which knew his own,
    But sighs at his untimely end ;
There is no heart, however lone,
    But feels the loss of such a friend.

He had a heart could feel and care
    For others when misfortune came ;
He had a hand as free to share,
    Which gave to him an honoured fame

But now he sleeps the sleep of death,
    While weeping friends around him stand ;
No tears can give life back his breath,
    Nor sighs can move his generous hand.

On angels' wings, midst smiles of love,
    His soul in rapid flight they bore,
To meet departed ones above,
    And join where partings are no more.

That soul *may* watch in closeness by,
    To guard with care his orphan boy ;
His ear *may* hear the widow's sigh,
    Then softly whisper words of joy.

But earth with all its flowery meads,
    And sky with all its shining lights,
His eye no more their beauty heeds,
    Nor scans the lofty mountain heights.

But sweetly at the Saviour's feet—
    That Saviour whom on earth he loved—
With white-robed ones he there will meet,
    Who faithful to God's word have proved,

'Then, if the gloomy grave has claimed
    The form whom all did fondly love ;
If with his zeal we are inflamed,
    We, too, shall share his prize above.

A HISTORICAL MEMORANDA.

*St. Cuthbert's Weather Cock was blown down November, 1872,
and replaced January 25th, 1873, by John Ives.*

'Tis fifty springs, since with golden wings,
    I stood in our Market Square ;
The people cheered, as my head I reared,
    To crow in the high mid air.
But the children then, are now grey old men,
    Who watched me on that day :
O, who will live an account to give,
    If to earth again I stray ?
The grand old spire they did admire,
    When to my roost I flew,
And I've kept my stand, high above the land,
    With my weather eye in view.

I've look'd o'er my wings, at wondrous things
    Since George the fourth did reign,
I saw from my nest a wondrous guest,
    They call'd a railway train.

Fatigue it ne'er showed, with its ponderous load,
  When down to the east it went ;
Not a few exclaimed, as it onward flamed,
  " That the dark one—evil meant."
(a) 'Twas old (No. 1) went puffing along
  So smoothly o'er the rail ;
And George from the North, who brought the thing
    forth,
  Said truly it ne'er would fail.

*A man of fame with a princely name
  I've seen the *special* bring ;
With power and might his princely right
  He ruled as railway king.
And his transcient sway, though for a day,
  Was felt the nation o'er ;
But now he's at rest, where the painless breast
  Can be disturbed no more.
(b) And I have seen our glorious Queen,
  As on the line she hied,
Give such a smile when for a while
  My golden wings she spied.
Young Albert sat with his feathered hat,
  As Princes sit in Wales ;
He danced when told, I was clad in gold,
  And weathered many gales.

(a) In 1825 the first locomotive engine ran on the Stockton and
Darlington Railway.
  *George Hudson.
(b) The Queen passed through Darlington on her way to Scotland, September 28th, 1849.

I remember well how the old church bell
    Rang loud for Sir Robert Peel,
As he rode with grace through the Market-place
    To speak of the people's weal ;
And how the cheer went up so clear
    When Kossuth came in sight ;
Like a champion brave he crossed the wave
    To share a Briton's right.

I saw from my stand a sight most grand
    As cheer on cheer rose high ;
(c) When thousands lined, and amply dined,
    Of English beef and pie ;
For old Earl Grey had swept away
    The cobwebs of the past !
And the great Reform had pass'd the storm
    And Britons freed at last.
Two gallant knights, for the people's rights,
    That year were safe returned ;
And the glowing fire of this southern shire
    In Pease and Bowes still burn'd.

One day in May I heard them say,
    The Town a Mayor should see ;
Not a few did say, they'd rue the day
    For who their Mayors should be.

(c) In 1832 a public dinner was given in the Market-place after
the passing of the Reform Bill.

(d) I saw from my station a real Corporation
    With Councillors new from the mint,
And I'm bound to believe, that no burgess will grieve,
    If you gave them a hint.
For a generous heart takes a noble part
    (e) In our honoured friend, the Mayor ;
And this good old town of Quaker renown,
    Will his gifts most freely share.

Now I heard from the *Times,* that the old clock chimes
    Again should sweetly play ;
How I'd clap my wing, could I hear them ring
    On some sweet summer day.
They would cheer my heart, to take a part
    Through the cold and winter rain,
And the young would sing when they heard them ring
    Their merry merry strain.

From my stand on high, my best I'll try,
    To tell how blows the wind ;
And I humbly trust no sudden gust
    Will prove to me unkind ;
For my body lay, 'mong the tombs one day,
    And I nearly had expired,
But they brushed my comb, and sent me home,
    To the place I most desired.

    (d) Darlington was made a Corporate Town, 1867.
    (e) Alderman Luck, Mayor for 1873.

PRIMROSES.

Brightest gems of the sunlit brow,
Strung with pearls of the morning dew,
Fresh from the Great Creator's hand,
Like jewels from the glory land.

Those flowers—so rich, so fresh and wild—
Once cherished by the Saxon child,
As through the forest tracks he stroll'd,
When spring had changed from Winter's cold.

And English children love them still,
Who watch them on the sloping hill;
They think of ages now no more,
When Alfred ruled this sea-girt shore.

Those flowers—so full of verdant bloom,
Prized for their rich and rare perfume—
With hues so sweet, so soft and fair,
They seem to lighten every care.

The mystic leaves which shield the flower,
And shelters in the storm-toss'd hour;
Remind the heart how sure and true
God watches all life's journey through.

When sinks the soul with sorrow down,
You look upon its star-deck'd crown;
'Tis like a gentle soothing word,
And joy from grief is soon restored.

Some unseen angel with his wing
Hath surely tipp'd this flower of Spring,
And left a fragrance, pure and sweet,
Beneath his swift angelic feet.

O lovely flower, how fair thy form,
How welcome after Winter's storm ;
How full of beauty, full of grace,
Is every line of thy fair face !

We love thee as we love the Spring,
Thou sweet and lovely little thing,—
For all thy nature tells of love,
Bursting from that Power above.

Now when these flowers their leaves shall fold,
And shrivel with the Winter's cold,
Others again shall fill their room,
For Spring will make the Primrose bloom.

MOULTON MANOR HOUSE, YORKSHIRE.

'Twas winter, and the driven snow
　　Lay deep around the Manor site,
And fair Cynthia shone below
　　With her ethereal beams of light.

The grey old house, with terrac'd wall,
　　Look'd grim amid this winter scene,
With pearl-white carpet round withal,
　　Where once it stood 'mid one so green.

The peering stars shone softly down
　　Like spangled gold on garments white—
Or like some bright imperial crown
　　Starr'd with diamonds clear and bright.

The merry laugh from forms within,
　　Who sat around the blazing fire,
Betokened that no feudal din
　　Had stirred to wrath the chieftain's ire.

Here often in the days of yore
　　Fair maidens deck'd this ancient pile
With mistletoe and festive store
　　As Christmas days grew on awhile.

The holly branch, the drooping yew,
　　The ivy leaf, the winter rose
Were ranged to give a pleasing view
　　To happy scenes of sweet repose.

The stalwart youth, the stately maid,
　　The thoughtful sire of riper years,
Have in these walls a tribute paid
　　To Father Christmas and his peers.

The bounteous stores has here been spread
　　With dainties for the festive scene;
The flavour'd game, the boar's grim head,
　　With many a racy dish between.

Bright visions too have fill'd each heart,
　As round the board the guests were placed,
While joyous songs have been the part
　Of maidens fair with sweetness graced.

When summer flowers in colours rare
　Bedeck'd the grounds of this domain,
Gay damsels void of thought or care,
　Tripp'd o'er the grassy lea and plain.

There filled with sportive life they danced,
　While plum'd knights on chargers bright,
So swift of foot, have plunged and pranced,
　As if in dance they took delight.

Now maidens and their lovers sleep,
　Whose voice once echo'd through these walls;
Yet memory o'er their deeds would keep
　A record which old Time recalls.

Dim shadows of the misty past
　But faintly picture out its fame,
While history's light is dimly cast
　O'er pages of its ancient name.

D

A DAY AT ULLESWATER LAKE.

High up among the mountains,
　And round the sombre lake,
Where gushing streams from fountains
　Such merry quivers make ;
Around the stately fir trees
　We'll wander far and near,
Like merry, buzzing wild bees,
　With nothing near to fear.

There odours on soft breezes
　Are wafted swiftly by,
With everything that pleases
　A child of nature's eye.
Wild flowers are brightly growing
　Where ferns lift up their heads,
And pearly streams are flowing
　Between their grassy beds.

We'll bask beneath the sunshine,
　We'll breathe the mountain air ;
For it's the merry hay time,
　When all is fresh and fair.
We leave earth's cares behind us
　For pleasures such as these.
And nature's hand will find us
　Her treasur'd stores to please.

Our leader we will follow,
　Where trip the fallow deer,
Near trees with ages hollow
　Through many a weary year.
We'll wander by the lake side,
　Where young feet trod before,
Where crystal streams run deep and wide
　Along its silent shore.

On cliffs beyond the grey hills,
　The great Helvellyn reigns;
A monarch who with awe fills
　His subjects on the plains.
He stands a proud imperial,
　Like some great star of state,
And yet its immaterial
　The forms he may dictate.

'Mid such a spot as this is
　The heart with joy is full;
Where all a perfect bliss is
　What soul could here be dull?
Yon ancient tower and woodland
　Are glorious to the sight,
We'll call it Cambria's good land,
　The scene's so fair and bright.

The Swiss may praise their Tyrol,
　And Italy laud its Rome,

But we prefer a day's stroll
　Among our lakes at home.
They are by far the neatest,
　Mid mountains, bold and grand,
And landscapes far the sweetest
　Of any foreign land.

Its meadows here are greenest,
　With heather hills and vales,
Where cottages the cleanest
　Are scattered through their dales.
The sky seems here the clearest,
　When clouds are cast aside,
To British hearts the dearest,
　To nature's child a pride.

But Sol with gold is gilding
　The mountain's peering head,
As o'er the eagles building
　His golden beams are shed ;
Our footsteps we'll retrace then,
　And bid each spot adieu,
For such a glorious place then
　Earth's treasures have but few.

THE YOUNG LIFE.

AN ACROSTIC.

As the young blossoms on the tree
Remind us what our life may be,
Telling that as they may yield
Harvest fruit from flower or field ;
Unless some sad untimely blow,
Reduce them with the frost and snow,
How charmed is life, in childhood's days,
Elastic, full of pleasing ways,
Ne'er dreaming that it e'er will glide
Round jutting rocks, where dangers bide ;
Yes, play they on from morn till eve,
Heedless, as if none would deceive.
O may that life so young and fair
Receive from heaven the Father's care,
So may it reap in riper years
Love and truth and filial fears ;
E'en then may grace a harvest bear,
Yielding fruit with saints to share.

MUSIC'S MUSINGS.

Mary sit down and tune the lyre,
While Lilly cheers us with the fire ;
Then John will sing his favourite song
He used to sing so sweet and long.

That song he calls " The Distant Shore,"
I love the thoughts yet more and more ;
They touch the feelings of the mind
In words pathetic, sweet and kind.

And Charley, you can take a book,
And o'er its pages keenly look ;
You always like some touching tale,
Which Scottish bards in verse detail.

'Twill make you think of friends away,
When in school days you used to play
Around the joyous village green,
Where many a merry heart was seen.

And I will listen to the notes,
As through the room the music floats,—
Sweet chords that seem to melt the heart,
And tender sympathies impart.

When young, I always loved to hear
The chords of music on my ear,
And now that years have changed my hair,
Still for its sounds I love and care.

I know that Autumn leaves do fall
And rustle by the garden wall ;
I know that flowers, however sweet,
Will fade and dangle at the feet.

1 know that stars, however bright,
Will fade when comes the morning light ;
I know that songs will have an end,
And partings come to every friend.

And music that our spirits charm,
Which gives to life a love so warm,
May still be heard upon the ears
In the long and distant years.

How oft in Spring the bloom is seen
Ere yet the leaves have come out green,
And fruit a prize has proved to be,
When leaves have left the parent tree.

So may it be when life shall end,
That branches may with burdens bend,
And loving ones with joy may see
The fruit that graced the parent tree.

But endings come to everything—
E'en to the sweetest songs we sing,
And moaning winds which breezes sigh
Will tremble out the notes, good bye !

Then sing that song, " The Distant Shore,"
It seems to charm me more and more,
And in some lonely hours of night,
May give to memory sweet delight.

ON THE DEPARTURE OF BRITISH TROOPS FROM PORTSMOUTH FOR AFRICA.

The sound of martial music sweet
Was heard within the crowded street,
Where Britain's sons, in bright array,
Were gathering for the parting day.
There brave men marched with steady step,
Obedient to their leader's beck,
While many a loud and hearty cheer
Burst from the crowd as they drew near.
But few could read the soldier's heart,
The saddened thoughts which formed a part
Of keen emotions lying there,
In bosoms fill'd with anxious care.
For from the breast there rose a sigh—
Not that the soldier feared to die,
But that full soon the tender tie
Which binds the heart and cheers the eye
Would broken be, and leave a blank
On every soul within the rank ;—
Some tender maid be left behind,
Where love's affections were entwined—
Some loving wife, and children too—
Some mother's smile, some cottage view.
These in his pensive soul would start,
And rack the mind—for they must part ;

No hearts were light when sisters press'd
And clung upon the soldier's breast.
Who could such waves of sorrow stand
When fathers clasp'd the soldier's hand?
Who in the thousands gathered here
Could help to shed one parting tear?
No eloquence could give relief
To parting wives bow'd down with grief,
When from the ranks their burdens bore,
From those perchance they'd see no more.
For in those climes where Zulus horde
They there might fall, though not with sword.
O ! that the white flag high was reared,
Replacing that with blood besmeared,
Then peaceful times a joy would yield
More glorious than the battle field,
No more to mourn the dying brave
Who found an Isandula grave.

ON KIRKE WHITE AND SHELLEY.

To thee, Kirke White, whose loftly soul
Could all thy gifted thoughts control,
And wing like eagle bird for flight
O'er regions of the starry night;
To thee I sing a poet's song,
And warble out in notes full long

The triumphs of thy youthful day,
And sigh, thy soul should pass away,
And leave us when thy morning star
Was shining in bright regions far,
Till morning's dawn and its bright cloud
Wrap'd thee within its whitened shroud.
Yet though so young, and though so bright,
Thy mind knew nought of mist or night,
For thy young soul had learn'd to prize
The gifts that lay beyond the skies ;
And God and truth thy heart obeyed,
And all thy moral virtues swayed,
E'en now like incense burning bright
Shall be the young heart's dear delight.

Would that young Shelley could have steered,
When adverse winds his frail barque veer'd,
And through the stormy seas of life
Sail calm o'er its fierce waves of strife.
If sceptic thoughts bedimmed thy mind,
Thy loftly soul could surely find
Some dashing force, some power to bear,
And let them float on passing air.
Thy passioned soul could mount on high
Like summer birds toward the sky,
And with their bright and fluttering wings
Scan nature with its thousand springs.
The passing cloud might oft obscure
Thy onward path from things so pure,

And dim the visions of thy soul
When doubts and fears would it control.
Thy intellect of empire thought
Had by illumined learning taught ;
O, that thy star had shone as bright,
Poor Shelley, with thy blaze of light,
As he who struggled with disease,
Yet grasped the truth with child-like ease.
So would thy star enlighten still
The grasping mind and ardent will,
And in thy love for lore and fame
Left blazing forth an honoured name.

THE MERRY DAYS OF SKATING.

See the merry youngster's glide
    O'er the crisp and silv'ry ice,
Each with wonted meed of pride,
    Cutting airs of strange device.

Laughing maids with merry hearts
    Dashing at a flying speed,
Tripping, chipping in all arts,
    Never seeming to take heed.

Now and then a bounce they gave, .
    Not designed ; of course, 'twas not ;
Maiden hearts are always brave,
    They ne'er think of such a plot.

But the gallant and the gay,
　　Who the rescued ones embrace,
Carry off their willing prey
　　To another skating race.

Thus the skating sport goes on
　　Through the chilly winter day,
Warm'd as if the tropic sun
　　Had been shining all the way.

Gliding swiftly, chatting free,
　　O'er the glassy ice they go,
Merry souls they seem to be,
　　Full of life and full of glow.

When the ice to waters flow,
　　Passing with the changing tide,
Then to other sports they go,
　　Closer by each other's side.

Honeymoons beam out above
　　In the clear ethereal sky,
For the young have learn'd to love
　　On the ice as they pass'd by.

Hearts are warm, cares are light,
　　Like the early blush of morn,
When it leaves the darksome night
　　Hills and valleys to adorn.

May each life like crystal be
    Clear as ice that bore them on,
From life's woes be ever free
    When the winter days are gone.

TO A YOUNG LADY.

A maiden sat in sweetness by
With smiling face and sparkling eye,
Her heart was full of tender thought
As through the cells, the passions wrought,
They rose like incense to the sky
Though none could see them passing by,
Like ether from some chemist's vial
Or shocks from some magnetic pile,
Now who could tell her heart's loud beat?
Or who could pierce its sacred seat?
Those eyes that flashed seraphic fire
Betoken'd some divine desire,
Or they may of a truth unfold
Some precious gift more prized than gold,
Concealed from those who round her move,
Prized treasures of an ardent love,
Which in some hour of great unrest
Will pass into another's breast;
And just as flowers their fragrance yield
Will perfume some young lover's shield—

Which through life's path of light and shade
Will gladden where devotion's paid.
And so that merry little heart
Will to the world a joy impart ;
And those who in her presence dwell,
Will see her smiles, dark clouds expel :
O ! happy he who wins her life,
O ! happy he with such a wife.

CLEOPATRA'S NEEDLE.

Hail ! monument of her, whose mighty name
Gave Egypt to the world so great a fame,
Who lured the Roman from his distant shore,
And stripp'd him of the honours that he bore.
No monarch ruled like her, with power so great,
Where once the Pharaohs reigned in pomp and state ;
Whose cities dazzled all the world awhile,
Where flowed the waters of the ancient Nile.
This empire Queen, so famed for lore and wit,
Shone like some star with bright effulgence lit :
No power, though strong, her mandates could with-
    stand ;
She ruled o'er Egypt with Imperial hand.
Yet, ere withal, she sought her people's good.
And for her nation's weal she bravely stood,
Till in temptation's dark and fitful hour,
She faded like some gay and gorgeous flower ;

Sad news of her Antony's fate was spread,
And in her inmost heart she mourned him dead,
Then with her hand the deadly asp applied,
And, 'mid the wailings of her people, died.
So Egypt mourn'd their Queen's untimely fate,
Yet strove to keep by fame a name so great,
That Time's rough hand through ages still might bear
The tribute of a love deep chisell'd there.
Proud Egypt had in generations past
Rear'd to her kings a token that would last ;
The pyramids, the mammoth sphinx's head,
Were memoirs of their great and cherish'd dead :
So their lov'd Queen, these people of the Nile,
Immortalized her name in true Egyptian style,
Which through encycled ages still remains,
While homes once fair lie levelled with the plains ;
And empires that have flourished ages long,
Whose peoples did their mighty cities throng,
Have to oblivion's boundaries pass'd away,
With cherished treasures left to Time's decay,
And this old granite* from her desert plains
A wonder to this wondrous age remains ;
And now amid old Albion's treasures stand
This relic of an ancient classic land,

---

* This Obelisk, which two thousand years before, graced the
city of the sun, had been brought to Alexandria to adorn the
entrance of Cleopatra's Palace, was brought over through the
engineering skill of Mr J. Dixon, C.E., at the expense of
Erasmus Wilson, and erected on the Thames Embankment, 1878.

Close by where Thames in its quaint way rolls by,
Far distant from the Heliopolien sky ;
Long may it stand within this sea-girt isle,
Proud emblem of Egyptian art and style.

DIED AT HIS POST.

The sun shone on the old church spire
   With a rosy-tinted ray,
As if St. Cuthbert with his fire
   Had gone within to pray.
The old clock ticked as it had done
   For many years before,
The quiet dead, whose race was run,
   Slept as if they'd wake no more.

The old bells hung in silence too,
   'Twas early Sabbath morn,
And worshippers were but few
   To sing their praise in turn.
The welcome notes of sounding bells
   Had not as yet been heard,
Which their soft music sweetly tells
   Of joy their sounds afford.

But, hark ! their changes now are rung,
   Their sounds are on the breeze,
And worshippers in numbers throng
   To bend in prayer their knees.

But as these trembling accents died
  On this sweet Sabbath day,
This aged ringer faintly sighed,
  Then passed to bliss away.

His last ring was to call to prayer,—
  To Temples built with hands,
That all might sweetly worship where
  The earthly Temple stands.
No more on Sabbath days he'll ring,
  As he has rung before,
But with the saints will sweetly sing
  Where bells are heard no more.

Mr. T. Preston, who was a bell-ringer for sixty years, died suddenly whilst ringing in St. Cuthbert's beltry, on Sunday morning, October 6th, 1872, at the age of 85.]

THE BOULDER STONE, NORTHGATE,

COMMONLY CALLED "*BULMER'S STONE."

There's a strange old stone on the old North-road,
From the granite hills, quite a giant's load,
Which some glacier left on its onward flow,
Away from its bed of eternal snow.

* Some forty years ago, the governors of the town, called "Town Commissioners," thought the stone was in the road of passers by, and gave orders for its removal. The venerable Edward Pease, whose house was nearly opposite, enquired what the men were going to do, and when told, said, "Take up your picks and spades, and off with you;" and he was right to preserve this geological wonder to Darlington.

'Twas in ages past, when a tidal wave
Came sweeping along this land of the brave.
In the times before men tilled virgin soil,
Or sweat on the brow by wearisome toil.
With billows that roll'd from a Greenland shore,
In an iceberg grasp, its huge burden bore.
The winds and the storm with their mighty force,
Rolled it o'er and o'er in their rugged course;
It's sides were shaped like a well polished sphere,
And left it quite safe, deeply submerg'd here,
Till the weary waste of the ocean stream
Through vast cycled ages—though just like a dream—
Left islands so fair, with mountains and dales,
With rivers and brooks, and soft sombre vales;
And amidst them all this wond'rous stone,
From the lofty mount of some frigid zone.
'Twas there when the saint with ladder so high
Dream'd that it reached from earth to the sky;
Or priests of old time, who crossed Jordan's ford,
When each left a stone their path to record.
'Tis a strange old stone, with a history as strange
As a meteor stone from some planet's range.
For when warriors came from Imperial Rome
To shelter their heads in the old Briton's home,
They marvelled to see, as they marched to the North,
Where this strange old stone could really come forth.
The old Druid priest, with feet yet unshod,
Stood suppliant here and bowed to his God,

With altar before, and victim upon
To atone for the deeds poor Britons had done.
The old Saxons, too, were as greatly amazed
As on its smooth face they eagerly gazed.
And in times gone by—in old monkish days,
When pilgrim-like—they passed by these ways,
They stood to behold, with staff in their hand,
This wondrous stone in this northern land.
When Pudsey came here St. Cuthbert's to build,
He too was surprised, and with wonder was filled.
And thousands yet more like Pudsey of old
Have gazed on this stone as if it were gold;
While many a youth have skipt it right o'er,
And played round its base for many an hour.
And men that pass by oft think of the fun
They had in their youth when school time was done;
And the matrons too, oft give it a glance,
And think when as girls they would skip round and
    dance.
Though now fill'd with care, the thought and the sight
Inspires their souls with increasing delight;
And still it will be when these pass away
Of this granite stone there'll be much to say.
Like tales of the Jews, the fathers would tell
To children who came into Canaan to dwell.
May no Corporate hand ever tempt to disturb
This gift of old Time, this marvellous curb;

And as Science increase and Art spreads its fame,
May Darlington share its part in the same,
And this stone be the seal on which to record
The power which Science and Art doth accord.

RABY.

The sun shed his rays o'er the Western sky,
And the North wind moan'd through the trees with a
    sigh,
While Raby's high turrets were tinged with the gold
That oft had emblazoned those turrets of old;
And the grand sturdy oaks, which centuries had known
As the trees of the forest, like cedars had grown;
While the beech and the ash and the silvery yew
In beauty and grandeur harmoniously grew.
The park, with its walks and terraces round,
Appeared to the eye like enchanted ground;
Its lakes flashed the rays of the bright setting sun
As in sweetness it told that its race was near run;
While the flowers of Spring, and the blossoms of May
In profusion grew round the castle so grey,
Prized dogs in the distance were howling out loud,
As if on the fox destruction they'd vowed;
But Reynard ran free through the bush and the breeze
As gay speckled birds o'er the tall towering trees.

Beyond the green meads of that spacious domain
Vast herds of red deer browsed down on the plain,
And gracefully moved on their fast fleeting feet,
O'er beautiful grounds in their favoured retreat.
But the prospect above, from its battlements high,
Was enhanced to the mind as it flashed to the eye,
For around and afar stood village and seat;
The old Norman Church, near to dwellings so neat,
Where enclosed in its walls the stained windows shed
A soft sombre light, o'er some effigy's head,—
Some peer, who once moved with a glad courtier's mien
O'er the broad lands of Raby, with pastures so green,
But now in the arms of dread death lies a prey:
Whom no anthem will touch, with its sweet, solemn lay.
Now grim grew the day, and dark came the night,
Yet the banqueting hall was a-glistening with light,
A change from the hills and the heather-clad moor,
Where the breeze was so brisk, and the air was so pure;
The fairest of women, with ease and with grace,
Were gathered around in that charm'd princely place;
And the nobles of birth, who high in their rank,
Paced by their fair forms with demeanour so frank;
While the plate of the Vanes, long treasured and prized,
Bespangled the tables which art had devised.
Now others sought out for diversified sights,
'Mid trophies once taken in chivalrous fights,—
Fair statues in marble, so true in their art,
And pictures which seemed real life to impart.

The Rose* who once ranged o'er Raby's strong-hold
Ne'er gazed on such treasures of silver and gold;
Nor Westmoreland's Earl, though so brave and so true,
Could ever command such rare arts to his view.
Yet how cold is the heart that cannot admire
The brightest of Roses in virtue's attire;
But history full well in bold truths doth record
The Rose that adorned her gay chivalrous lord
The pageant and glory that once was known there,
When feudal lords ruled as Czars only dare;
When the Nevilles with hawk, as falconers would try,
With maidens of birth to draw game from on high;
When yeoman and vassal were called forth to arms,
And blasts of the war-horn created alarms.
But these days of war-strife we hear now no more,
And struggles of chieftains none now need deplore;
Where war was once blighting, sweet peace takes the
        place,
And freedom's enjoyed by the great English race:
This relic remains a memorial of power,
With its high-crested wall and strong-tested tower,
And coroneted nobles in silence doth sleep,
Who once felt secure in their adamant keep.
Yet bold and majestic the old Castle stands,
In strength and in fame in these old English lands;
A marvel of skill and a wonder of art,
When barons around played so potent a part.

*The Rose of Raby is locally known as an historical novel,
and is much admired. Rose being the daughter of the great
Earl of Westmoreland.

THE SCHOOL MASTER'S REVERIE.

O, who can forget when life was but young,
When sweet flowers of hope round my pathway were
    strung,
When the leaf of the laurel, in the proud victor's crown,
I longed and I loved to call it my own.
The class were I stood, I remember it well,
How I struggled in everything to excel ;
The tasks I had learned, I mastered so true,
And looked on my plans, as to manhood I grew.
How I longed for the time to scatter the grain
I had stored in the cells of my young, thoughtful brain ;
How I tripp'd with light heart, when inspectors came
    round,
Like a merry, Spring lamb, I with gladness was found.
For I carried the prize, 'mid the shouts of the crowd,
And their praises for me were both boisterous and loud;
Those merry Spring-days I will never forget,
For such souls like my own I often have met ;
When, with frolicsome wit, and wisdom untried,
We each, with our knowledge of learning, have vied ;
Though the problems of Euclid puzzled my brain,
Yet I mastered them over and over again.
And the lustre which learning shed over my path,
I prized as a miser the treasures he hath.
Each school-day my mind sought for classical lore,
And the deeper I dug, I longed for the more ;

The keys that unlocked where fair knowledge was
    bound,
I grasped them with power, and their treasures I found.
The Iliad, the Ænead, and the poems of Greece,
I stored in my mind, and made knowledge increase ;
And now in the school like a monarch I sit,
Clothed in the purple of learning and wit,
Dispensing my store as my moments engage,
In learning the young of this wonderful age ;
For knowledge is power—may it flood the wide world,
And ignorance from hence for ever be hurled.

ON THE SABBATH NIGHT SERVICES,

IN CONNECTION WITH THE TEMPERANCE SOCIETY.

The stars in their glory above us shone bright,
Their sweet scintillations illumined the night,
The singers in Zion had finished their song
In the Temples below where the worshippers throng,
For the Sabbath had passed in its calmness away
Like a bright setting sun, with its gold-tinted ray.

But the workers had work ere their slumbers came on,
And they sighed at the doom of the poor erring one ;
They gathered around, where in hundreds they met,
To tell them of woes which no heart can forget.
And they prayed that the Church with its lever of love
Might help " Briton's curse " at once to remove.

O, sad was the tale which in sorrow they told
Of drunkards who strayed so far from the fold ;
And they prayed for the time when the demon of
    drink
Should for ever be chained with an adamant link,
That no more he might grasp the youth of our land
With his treacherous heart and his dark fiendish hand.

Poor drunkards lie down when the Sabbath is past,
While the sands of their life are running out fast,
They think not of Christ, who their ransom hath paid.
Whose life like a lamb on the altar was laid—
They've heard not the voice of the Saviour to say,
"Come, though poor lost one, to My fold come away.'

While those whom His hand should protect and
    provide,
Stand saddened and sorrowing close by his side ;
So pale and so weak—as if the Angel of Death
Had blown on that form with his withering breath ;
While the place they called home, might have smiled
    like the rose,
And been the sweet spot of a Christian's repose.

But they've drunk like a demon the poisonous cup,
To the home in the skies they've never look'd up ;
And their earthly home knows no comfort or bliss,
No smile for a wife—for the children no kiss.
And they pass thus away like a vision or dream,
And are lost to our view like a straw on the stream.

O ! Christians, tell them the fold is so free
There's room for the drunkard as well as for thee—
If he ceases to drink and comes to the Cross
His heart shall be changed like to silver for dross ;
And the house of the Lord will his praises resound :
When the drunkard is free, and the lost one is found !

BY WINDERMERE.

The sun was setting bright and fair
   O'er Langdale's steep and rugged height,
While fleecy clouds in soft mid air
   Were closing round the shades of night.

Deep shadows dimmed the mountain brow,
   The distant hills look'd grim and grey,
While silver streamlets in their flow
   Came dashing forth mid sparkling spray.

His golden rays streamed softly down
   O'er Loughrigg's steep and rock-bound side,
By sombre shades where mountains frown
   And sailing crafts so smoothly glide.

The Queenly Lake of Windermere
   Was gilded with his golden flame,
Till mount and hill were mirror'd clear
   As o'er their tops his flashes came.

Sweet Rydal saw his flushing face
   Though closed by hills and sylvan groves,
And laughing brooks caught his embrace
   Where round their edge the swallow hoves.

His rays lit up with golden sheen
   The top of Fairfield's towering head,
While Kirkstone with its pass between
   A magic glare of glory shed.

The British clans in days of yore
   Have wandered o'er those lofty hills—
By sylvan glades and moss-clad moor
   By flowing brooks and rippling rills.

Oft in their wildness they have strayed
   Both daring, dauntless, bold and free,
With fiery wills, have undismayed
   Ranged o'er those haunts where dangers be.

In distant times, the Romans too,
   Found homes around this solitude,
They kept the passes sure and true
   'Mid peoples brave, though counted rude.

The spots where they such power controll'd—
   Where Roman legions marched to war—
Are now the mountain-shepherd's fold
   With nought to harm and nought to mar.

Here many a knight in mail array'd
　　From castles grey, or baron hall,
Have with their plighted ladies stray'd
　　By mountain range and waterfall.

And we to-day have scann'd the heights
　　Our fathers trod in days gone by,
Who lov'd to sport in wild delights
　　By scenes, where now their ashes lie.

When winters come and summers go,
　　As fleeting time flies on the wing—
When these high cliffs are capt with snow,
　　Or summer birds again shall sing.

Then other eyes these scenes will view—
　　Shall revel in their glowing sights,
And pleasure with its charms renew
　　What to the mind are pure delights.

THE SNOW-DROPS.

Beautiful snow-drops, gems of the year;
Welcome in winter, precious and dear.
Beautiful snow-drops, pure as the snow,
Come to enliven creatures below.

Beautiful snow-drops, pearls of the land,
Fresh as creation from the Lord's hand.
Beautiful snow-drops, in winter days,
Sent as a token to gladden our ways.

Beautiful snow-drops, just like the dawn
After the midnight gilding the lawn.
Beautiful snow-drops, drooping the head
Like little Cupids on a rose bed.

Beautiful snow-drops, who could compare
The price of a jewel to flowers so fair?
On small tender stems, heads hanging low,
Kissing the flakes of beautiful snow.

And when the snow melts, still they are seen,
Kissing the grass of beautiful green.
When spring-time shall come with gentle showers,
There never will come more beautiful flowers.

Beautiful snow-drops, my God hath given,
As pure as the flowers scatter'd o'er Heaven.
These then remind us God will still give,
A harvest of flowers long as we live.

DR. LIVINGSTONE, THE AFRICAN EXPLORER,

BORN IN SCOTLAND, 1815; DIED IN AFRICA, 1873.

A dark wave of sorrow has surged on our shore,
  For a prince has been pierced with the arrow of
    death;
The brave-hearted Livingstone is now no more,
  Who breathed for the African his very last breath.

He died on those plains where the tropical sun
    Pours down his bright beams on the African race,
Before the great work of their rights had been won,
    Or the chains which enthralled them were scattered
        apace.

He thirsted for good, as the roe thirsts for rain,
    That the dark spots of sin might be washed from
        the land;
That the curs'd crime of bondage might never again
    Defile the dark tribes with its demon-like brand.

His own native shores he loved as his life,
    And fain would have died, where its streams are so
        clear,
Where its banks are so green, and its pleasures so rife
    But he died in the land which his soul loved so
        dear.

The proud throbbing heart in the warrior's breast
    Beats high when he dwells on the battles he's won,
And he paints on his panel a warrior's crest,
    While his country applauds for the deeds he has
        done.

The patriot longs for the laurel of fame,
    When his people are free'd from the oppressor and
        foe ;
And he glories with pride in a patriot's name,
    Though crushed for a time by the enemies' blow.

Now his was a cause both glorious and bold,
   As step after step he pressed his lone way ;
And the end which he sought was more precious than
     gold,
   For it opened the path to a civilized day.

O ! proud is the nation that claimed him a son,
   No honour's too great to crown his vast deeds,
And proud is the world for the work he has done,
   In planting the cross with truth-loving seeds.

The cross was his flag, and his watchword was peace,
   As he pass'd over jungle, mountain, and lake,
That the tribes he so loved, might with blessings
     increase,
   And their idols and crimes for ever forsake.

The pestilent beds of the African soil,
   With dangers surrounding the slave-loving king,
Never daunted his heart, ne'er lessen'd his toil,
   While his angel-voice cried, good tidings I bring.

Poor martyr, he died 'mid the deserts of sand,
   Where no kindred could drop on his bosom a tear ;
Nor watch his great soul depart to that strand
   To receive the reward he had purchased so dear.

IN THIS LIFE.

[Suggested on witnessing a beautiful sunset from the
Darlington Cemetery.]

The golden stream of the setting sun
    Was flashing glory everywhere,
And distant scenes and fleecy clouds
    Were flaming with its dazzling glare.

The beauty of his golden light
    Was shining in the distance far,
And Nature looked as if no blight
    Could for a time man's pleasures mar.

So sweetly did all gleam and glow,
    And all things looked so calm around,
That heaven, for once, seem'd here below,
    And man a paradise had found.

Just then a form, with saddened heart,
    Was bending o'er a new-made grave,
When grief afresh from wounds did start,
    Because she mourn'd a son so brave.

She watched him when in infant life
    He cheered her with his merry laugh ;
She loved him true, 'mid earth's rude strife,
    And thought he'd be in age her staff,

But sorrow bent that shrunken form
　While burning tears fell on that grave ;
She looked like one amid the storm
　When sinking in the yawning wave.

However fair life's scenes may be,
　A mantle comes like silent night ;
And things we loved and longed to see
　Are hidden from our mortal sight.

A little maiden with a flower
　Came near to where her mother sleeps,
And placed it on the shrouded bower
　Of her whose soul the Saviour keeps.

No mother now to see that sun
　Send down his streaming rays of gold,
Nor tell what wonders it had done,
　Since blushing morn, through space it roll'd.

How often life is mixed with woe,
　Though nature smiles like spring's fair morn,
And when we'd pluck the flowers that grow
　How oft we feel a piercing thorn.

When silver streams from fountains gush,
　And balmy breezes fill the air ;
O who could dream when hearts are flush,
　That there was sighing anywhere.

'Tis strange that in this mortal vale,
   When beauty gilds the path of light,
Some sudden and unwelcome tale
   Should change our bliss, like mists at night.

The fairest flowers of earth do fade,
   The brighest day returns to night ;
And stars of hope, like evening's shade,
   Have pass'd away from mortal sight.

But fields and flowers and streams of light
   In life beyond, ne'er pass from view ;
No shadows of a darksome night
   No setting sun, no evening dew.

BLENCATHRA ;

OR SADDLEBACK, CUMBERLAND.

The foe had encamped 'neath the heather-clad hill,
While the pale crescent moon shone so peerless
   and still ;
And the shadow of mighty Blencathra was seen,
Stretching its form o'er the valleys so green.
On far-distant hills flamed the beacons of light,
'Mid the blaze of the stars on that sweet autumn night ;
And the rippling stream sung in wildness away
Its vigils so sweet at the close of the day.

Enshrined in the cliff where the still waters lay,
Where solitude heightens the gloom on its way;
There the sweet bride of Derwent, so pale and so fair,
Escaped from her lord and found sure refuge there.
The monk of St. Herbert had steered o'er the wave,
And prayed the return of that champion so brave.
And he came as the light of the morning came forth,
With his beautiful bride from the cliffs of the North;
The dew of Blencathra shone on her brown locks
Like the pearls that hang on the fleece of the flocks;
For the foeman had gone on his errand of death,
Breathing out woe from his flame-tainted breath.
But the lord of the Isle had escaped from his hand, .
And gathering friends in his fair presence stand;
They exultingly cheer as their banner they lift,
And crown the fair one with a garlanded gift;
For the daughter of birth hath been spared once again
And they sing a sweet song in a still sweeter strain,
E'en the solitary place where in anguish they strayed
Through the lone hours of night as each one had
        prayed;
E'en there the faint accents like music is heard,
So softly to echo the voice of her lord;
And the tarn of Blencathra, though lone as the grave;
Seems to murmur an echo, all peace to the brave.
Now when summer days come and the heather's in
        bloom,
And the wild flowers fill the air with perfume.

And the spiral leaf of the beautiful fern
On the heights of Blencathra its summits adorn.
Then the young and light-hearted climb on its brow;
In sweet-sounding words they also do vow
They'll shelter each other 'mid struggles for life,
When foes, like the world, surround them in strife.

THE LITTLE MAIDEN AND THE FLOWERS.

A little maiden smiled with joy
Because the days of spring had come ;
She wandered forth among the flowers,
And with her hand she gathered some.

'Twas sweet to see her little form,
As o'er the grassy lawn she hied ;
And how her little heart did beat
When fragrant violet flowers she spied.

She gathered forth those gems of spring,
So soft, so sweet, so wondrous made,
And in her little tiny hands
An offering to her teacher paid.

'Twas hard to say which looked the best,
The flowers or her who offered them ;
For both were soft, and sweet and fair—
Each sparkled like a polished gem.

Sweet innocence marked every flower,
Sweet fragrance came from every leaf;
For God had stamped his image there,
Though life in flowers may be but brief.

O glorious flowers from heath or wood,
We hail you as a welcome guest;
Ye gladden many a dreary path,
Ye soften many a troubled breast.

Though earth has many a gloomy spot,
With many a barren waste around,
Yet many a sweet forget-me-not
There still may on its wilds be found.

Then praise to Him who made the flowers,
And offers them as with a smile;
Yea, praise to that Eternal One,
Who brightens up man's path awhile.

"HE CARETH FOR ME."

(Written after hearing a Sermon by the Rev. Arthur Hands,
from the above Text.)

Though dark the path my feet have trod,
And weak and pained I'd weary be,
I knew the great Jehovah-God
Did hourly watch and care for me.

When sorrow's tears bedimm'd my eye
For friends I loved but could not see,
I knew that One was always nigh
Who look'd and truly cared for me.

He watches every flower that grows,
He curbs the deep and stormy sea,
On all His works He care bestows ;
Then surely He will care for me.

When instinct was the guiding power,
My infant days were pleased to see,
The Father watched through every hour,
E'en then, I know, he cared for me.

And now that manhood's days have come,
When cares of life cleave fast to me,
I know, however great their sum,
My Father still doth care for me.

When sunk my soul and pain'd my heart,—
When earthly comforts from me flee,
Yet He doth kindly aid impart,
Because He loves and cares for me.

If my lone soul, like some frail barque,
Is tossed upon life's checkered sea
Without a star my path to mark,
I know a steersman cares for me.

Though death's dark valley I may tread,
No light around that I may see,
There's One, who conquering hosts have led
Through vales as dark, who cares for me.

I know that far beyond this shore,
'Mid scenes of sweet serenity,
His blessed hand will give the more,
Who here so kindly cares for me,

————

DEEPDALE.

*A lovely Rural Scene near Barnard Castle, stretching over which
is a beautiful Viaduct.*

Let me sing of thy charms, thou green garland dale,
Where no heart can be sad, no pleasure can fail;
For the bright flowers of Spring in innocence grow
'Mid thy clear sparkling streams, as onward they flow.
Thy banks are all green, and thy borders all gay,
With the jessamine bud and the sweet-scented May;
Those bright little gems—the heather blue-bell,
The yellow primrose and the red pimpernell—
The feather-shaped fern, with the choicest of flowers,
Are crowding around these wild wooded bowers,
The rippling stream o'er the rugged cascade
Refreshes each flower and sprinkles each blade,
And gives to fair Nature a charm to sustain,

Who, knowing its bliss, would return there again.
Fair nymphs from the crowd have oft wandered out
    here,
Where the breeze is so fresh and the sky is so clear ;
Where the gallant and brave and true-hearted knight
Has cross'd the dark Tees from Barnard's rude height,
When the moon with her silvery beams shone so clear
On his glittering mail as he passed the red deer ;
While the dim tower of Baliol faded away,
Though the torch burnt so bright, from his lady so gay.
And the beacon-crowned cliff, with the maiden forlorn,
Who waved her pale light and beckoned his return.
But these chivalrous days have now pass'd away,
And the castle is crumbling fast to decay ;
But the glen and the dale are as bright as before,
And Nature has left us no past to deplore,
For its banks are as sweet, and its flowers are as gay,
As when falconers sought in its forests a prey.
And young ones and old may here still enjoy
The smiles of its stream, with none to annoy ;
And the lover of Nature may bow at its shrine,
Where the deep-seated roots of the old oaks entwine,
And sweetly look up to that Power above,
Who made every vale, and floods them with love.

THE FALLS OF LODORE.

See from yon steep and rugged height
   The mighty rush of waters roll;
Dashing and dancing with delight,
   As they approach the boiling goal.

Thy shaded streams, thou dark Lodore,
   Move swiftly on, like angels' feet—
At first they gently seem to stir,
   Then rush, the rock-bound foe to meet.

None daunted with the opposing one,
   They strengthen in their might and power,
Till swelling like deep chords in song,
   Above the calm of eve's still hour.

The rocks, which in confusion lie,
   Would stay them in their onward course;
But frowning barriers, they defy,
   And mock them with their mighty force.

While from thy lofty mountain form,
   In foaming streams they onward go;
Raging like furies in the storm,
   Till in serener paths they flow.

Their music fills the vales around,
   As thunders on the storm-toss'd air;
And mountains echo back the sound
   In notes entrancing, sweet and fair.

The sunlight gilds thy streams with gold,
  As o'er these craggy rocks they sport ;
Thy sprays, like silver mantles, fold
  Their beauty o'er the rock-bound fort.

Till Derwent, with its glossy face,
  Waits like a mother for her child,
And with her loving arms embrace
  The infant stream, now calm and mild.

Though dark thy waters, O Lodore,
  And wild the wreaths that deck thy brow
Who would not love thee more and more,
  When thy enchanting scenes they view?

Within your shrouded shades of wood,
  The footprints of a God are seen—
Teaching lessons pure and good
  To all who will His bounties glean.

My senses revel at the sight
  Of this proud spot of Nature's power,
Where majesty and marvellous might
  Has furnished such a gorgeous bower.

ON SCIENCE AND RELIGION.

When Science dawn'd, as doth the light,
  Amid the encircling mists of morn,
With faint outlines to human sight,
  For after ages to adorn.

The Pyramidical land gave birth
  To problems deep, with studied thought,
And with its learning opened forth
  The wonders which deep learning wrought.

The world of Nature lay conceal'd,
  Enshrouded in its native soil,
Till with their power they thus reveal'd
  The wonders of their mental toil.

The noble minded of Greek's sons,
  Though rul'd with philosophic thought,
Pursued the path where Science runs,
  And in their course fresh marvels wrought.

When Science on her fleetest wing,
  Soars out to regions yet untold ;
When men of thought their wonders bring,
  And marvels of research unfold ;

Men deem Religion doom'd to nought,—
  That all the yearnings of the heart,
And all the good by wisdom wrought,
  Will from man's inner life depart.

Why should the thought for once exist,
　　That Science should dim Religion's rays?
That it should cast o'er it a mist,
　　And sadden down men's faithful ways?

Let Lyell, Tyndall, and their kind,
　　With all the works their heads conceived,
Still bring before the searching mind
　　The wondrous triumphs they've achieved.

What truths the age of rocks unfold,
　　What mysteries deep in Nature dwells;
They've led the thoughtful to behold,
　　And search where God in power excels.

The world needs light to see God's skill
　　Developed in His wide domains,
To catch some glimpse of His great will,
　　Where Nature in her glory reigns.

His footprints teach us more and more,
　　As down the streams of time we glide,
To worship Him, and still adore
　　The power that in His works abide.

Then in the world there's room for each—
　　For Science and Religion too;
That mortals, God's great laws may teach,
　　And goodness through life's days pursue.

WORSHIP.

Written on crossing the North Sea, Sunday, August 10th, 1879.

'Tis sweet to sit beneath the vault
   Of God's eternal dome,
And worship at the mercy seat
   With those that's nearer home.

The mighty deep, with ceaseless song,
   Sends forth its chorus true,
Whilst His great ruling orb of light
   Rolls midst eternal blue.

In ages past Thy creatures all
   Have felt the power we feel,
When looking on the wondrous works
   On which God stamp'd His seal.

How great the power that rules the waves,
   That sets on them, a bound,—
We'd worship then that loving God
   Whose wisdom is profound.

He can protect on sea and shore
   Who holds them in His hand,
Then those are safe who trust His word,
   On seas or on the land.

So when the voyage of life shall end,
   And all its waves shall cease,
May we arrive within the port
   Where all is calm and peace.

WESTMINSTER ABBEY.

Strange thoughts steal o'er my soul to-day,
As through this ancient pile I tread,
Not that the sacred temple rears
To heaven its chaste and gothic head ;

But this inspires my wondering mind,
When through these dwellings of the dead,
With veneration and with awe,
I o'er their resting places tread,

'Tis true, that on this narrow spot,
The fabric of our fathers stand,
Among the grandest and the best,
Of this our dear old fatherland.

While he who lined, and he who built,
Alike have pass'd life's bounds away ;
In centuries gone, yet still their work
Is marvellous to the eye to-day.

The noble-minded of our race,
Lie sleeping in death's slumbers here ;
Who shaped the destinies of men—
The patriot, poet, and the peer.

The crumbling dust of mighty kings,
Who once for pageantry and show,
On battle-fields, in distant lands,
Made blood in streams profusely flow.

And queens, who with ambition swayed
Their sceptre o'er this glorious land ;
While monarchs trembled at the beck,
Of their Imperial, jewel'd hand.

A few are loved by some to day—
Good Eleanor, whose honoured name,
For Christian deeds is still enbalmed
In English hearts with lasting fame.

But few who wore a diadem,
Could truly boast of such a fame,
Their deeds are better dead than known,
For royal pomp is but a name.

The records of the mighty dead,
Whose monuments around me stand,
Shall far outlive the marble busts
Of men who trod this classic land.

Methinks that when the angel's trump
Shall waken up the silent dead,
That hosts within this sacred pile
Will rise as champions from their bed.

Brave Livingstone, who trod alone
O'er Afric's parched and sandy plain,
Shall, for his great and noble deeds,
A fadeless crown of glory gain.

The brightest of our English bards,
Who shone like guiding stars on high ;
Whose clear and radiant genius blazed
Along the dark and ebon sky.

Here Grey, who in elegiac verse
So touched the chords, that even now
We hear the music, soft and sweet,
Vibrating from his hallow'd yew.

Here Campbell, too, who sweetly sung,
And Johnson, of the poets rare ;
And Spencer, with his " Fairy Queen "—
These all a nation's homage share.

Here Chaucer, Southey, Spencer,
Goldsmith, and other illustrious men,
Who more than monarchs, with their rule,
Have reigned o'er empires with their pen.

Here Dryden, Addison, and Gay,
And Milton, too, in glory vie ;
Who wrote in epic verse sublime,
Though dark the vision of his eye.

If God has given to earth such gifts,
Will they not rule in higher spheres?
Where truth transcendent shines so bright,
And glory evermore appears.

Those mighty men with thought matured,
Will rise and shine supremely bright;
. Like stars of heaven's first magnitude,
In the celestial realms of light.

How proud the nation that can boast
Of minds so great and hearts so free,
Who leave behind such treasured lore,
For coming minds to grasp and see.

Yea, rich the isle that gave such sons,
Who paved the path to mighty fame,
Who bore on high the torch of truth,
And gave to earth their thoughts and name.

THE AUSTRIAN OFFICER AND HIS COUNTRY'S FLAG.

AN INCIDENT IN THE PRUSSIAN WAR.

The gloomy smoke of the battle field
Rose densely on the evening air,
And streams of light from distant stars
Shone dimly where the wounded were.

The broken lance and the lifeless lay
Where conflicts raged so wild and fierce,—
And young and brave ones slept a sleep
The trumpet's shrill notes could not pierce.

G

The wounded thought of home so dear
Some bent the knee as if in prayer,
While others lay in death's firm grasp—
Left in the gloom of dark despair.

And night clouds followed those of smoke,
And night dews those of shot and shell;
And friend and foe co-mingled lay,
For night had closed, and none could tell.

When morning broke with ruddy beams,
And virgin light shone on each form,
Thousands had slept the sleep of death—
Had fallen in the battle's storm.

When lo, a youth in Austrian mail,
Lay dying where the slain ones lay;
His eyes were fixed on his fatherland,
Though home and friends were far away.

A Patriot true, he'd fought and bled,
For home and for his country's laws;
And, as a hero, calmly dies,
So he died for its righteous cause.

'Mid dead and dying the Prussians sought
For those who before were deadly foes;
But moved with a soldier's pitying heart,
They seek to offer them repose.

They stooped and watched a dying youth;
They sought to bear his form away,
Where in their camp they might restore,
And to his lov'd one be a stay.

He heard them ask to save his life;—
Heard how each would his help bestow:
And when they asked again to move,
He look'd, yet firmly answered, "No."

Let us wait on him, then, for soon
He'll pass the portals of this state,
We'll bury him where he bravely fell,
For none, perchance, may know his fate.

And as they watched his sunken eye,
And smiles, which sweetly graced his brow;
Like a child as it sleeps, so he slept
On that sweet morning's early dew.

They gently raised his lifeless form,
When lo, on the dark and blood-stained dew,
There lay the flag where he had lain,
Concealed from the foeman's view.

High in the air, and through the storm,
He proudly bore his country's flag;
And when the fight in madness raged,
Through ranks of death his prize would drag.

'Till he fell on the field, when round
His form was wrapp'd, the flag of the brave;
Nor would he yield it up till he died—
When they carried him to a soldier's grave.

Let Christians firm and Patriots true,
Like heroes brave the truth uphold;
And never give up till the death-day comes,
Though offered a crown of the purest gold.

ENDYMION.

A shepherd whom Cynthia, in the classic age of Greece,
cast into a deep sleep that she might kiss him. Erato, the muse
who sings of love and marriage. Mythologically considered,
Endymion in a poetic sense, really refers to the setting of the sun
and rising of the moon amid his departing rays.

'Mid scenes of beauty, soft and fair,
Endymion paced with grace and ease;
While o'er his flocks with tender care
He watched beneath the shady trees.

Bright rosy tints, with golden hues,
Shone on those spots of classic Greece;
While wandering herds o'er pearly dews
Would there repose where all was peace.

Eve's courtly Queen, with silver veil,
Rose gently o'er the fleecy clouds,
Flooding with light the lonely dale,
Dashing aside the misty shrouds.

Fair Cynthia, like some modest naiad,
Beheld his young and lovely form ;
And from her heart she homage paid,
Pure as the breath of early morn.

The gushing springs of pent-up love
Burst from her soul's impassioned power ;
She stood as one who could not move
Beyond the verge of beauty's bower.

She felt the force of gold-winged love
Upheaving in her gentle breast,
Like the lone bird from heights above
Seeking a spot of quiet rest.

Fresh arrows pierced her inmost soul,
Firing her heart with force anew ;
And like a steed beyond control
Her onward course she would pursue.

Till sweet Erato, bright and fair,
In solitude stole softly by,
And saw sweet Cynthia, in despair,
Reasoning oft, and wondering why.

Then looking on the love-sick maid,
Whose tresses waved with night's soft breeze,
Her eyes on young Endymion stayed,
With thoughts within, but ill at ease.

Then with inspiring voice, she sang,
While sweet Erato strung her lyre,
Till all around with music rang,
Melodious as a seraph choir.

The magic of their cordant sound,
Entranced the shepherd's listening ear ;
Till with her charms he, dreaming, found
The lovely nymph reclining near.

Then with lips like leaves of roses,
She gently pressed her's to his own,
To calm the breast where love reposes,
And sweetly join their hearts in one.

And thus the young have found it so,
In every age, in every clime,
Emotions pure from hearts to flow,
And true as beats the pulse of time.

Thus early dreams, and love's first charms
Have lived through long and wearied years ;
While hope and love 'mid life's alarms,
Have dried up many a flood of tears.

As true as buds of early spring
Spread out their leaves with summer heat,
So early love its pleasures bring,
And helps to make life's joys complete.

IN MEMORIAM.

Written on the opening of the GURNEY PEASE'S MEMORIAL SCHOOL, Nestfield, Darlington. Erected by Mrs. G. Pease, as a memorial of her beloved husband who died in 1872. AGED 33 YEARS.

How sweet, when day declines and quiet eve
　　Throws its dim shadows o'er the mantled earth,
And star rays, like a monarch's jewelled crown,
　　Shine forth effulgently with priceless worth ;

When winter winds through creviced corners moan,
　　And all around, save these, are still as night—
How rich to be in solitude alone,
　　And feel the force of solitude's delight.

The fleeting shadows of the past come by
　　Like visions, in a sweet and soft repose,
When lov'd ones, who have gone to rest on high,
　　Come near awhile their treasures to disclose.

Fond memory grasps these greetings of the past,
　　For thoughts of them may surely never die,
No, long as reason reigns, they too will last,
　　Deep in the heart where evermore they lie,

Though feint the lines of life to us are seen,
　　And earthly care a time may these erase,
And be to us as though they ne'er had been,
　　Yet in the mind, their forms we still can trace.

The canvas of the heart can still portray
  The form and look of those we loved so well,
Though time, like summer dreams, pass swift away ;
  Their deeds we know in sweetest memories dwell.

The marbled tomb may state their age and death,
  And silver yew-trees guard their narrow bed,
And shelter those who quiet lie beneath ;
  But living hearts know best the lives they led.

We would not, therefore, grieve, that he has gone,
  For God who called him, is forever right—
The Father and the ever-loving one,
  He raised him far beyond the plains of night.

The widow's heart sometimes may feel forlorn,
  When orphans ask to have a father's smile ;
And loving friends betimes may weep and mourn,
  Because they cannot look upon his form awhile.

Who can forget his short, yet noble life,
  When battling for the right and human good ?
Who laid aside earth's busy scenes and strife.
  To give to youth the wealth of mental food.

And on the Sabbath, 'mid its holy hours,
  He lured the young to scenes more sacred still ;
Where, near the cross and aramanthine bowers,
  They soar'd within the gates on Zion's hilL

The good oft pass from loving life away
   Like flowers, yet seeds are scattered all around ;
And though their forms are lost by earth's decay,
   Like flowers they spring to beautify the ground.

How noble then, to have some record of the past—
   To silent speak the virtues of his mind—
A true memorial that long years may last,
   And be a blessing to the human kind.

'Tis not a temple reared to fading fame,
   Like Grecian ones, to deeds of cruel war.
Or reared to some heroic soldier's name ;
   'Tis one more glorious and more godly far.

ON THE DARLINGTON ATHLETIC
SPORTS.

In the palmy days of Greece,
   When her poets sought for fame,
When her glories did increase
   Through her exalted name.
She shone amid the splendour
   Of nations proud and brave,
And victory did attend her
   On land and on the wave.

Her temples shone with brightness
   Through all her sunny lands,
Reared with such taste and lightness
   By skill'd Athenian hands.
Her Gods look'd down upon her
   With smiles benign and sweet,
And nations gave her honour
   For glories so complete.

Her daughters were the fairest,
   And shone with such a grace,
That flowers which bloom'd the rarest
   Might vie with such a race.
Their eyes would pierce the night shade,
   However thick the gloom,
And yield to all a bright shade,
   Though leading to the tomb.

Her sons were bold and daring,
   They conquer'd in the fight ;
Few foes were found declaring
   To war against their might.
And when their victors landed
   And rode their cities through,
The laurel leaves were handed
   To crown each victor's brow.

In high days of their glory
   Those laurel leaves they gave

To Poets's for each story,
  And those they counted brave.
Her maids look'd on with pleasure
  When fleet ones ran so swift,
Then gave the laurel treasure
  To those who won the gift.

Vast throngs would watch with wonder
  The Gladiator's glance ;
The cheer, when broke asunder
  The famous foeman's lance.
Then came the gifts of honour
  For fair ones to bestow
On wrestler, or on runner,
  To crown the victor's brow.

Now Greece with all her glory,
  Her prowess and her name,
Is told in history's story
  With all their hero's fame.
Her laurel leaves have faded,
  Her heroes sleep in dust,
But Time's soft hand hath shaded
  What victors claimed so just.

Now Briton's sons are daring,
  Her swift athletes true,
The laurel leaves are waving
  Around their shining brow.

The fair ones, who beheld them,
  Press'd forward to the goal,
Gave prizes that propell'd them
  To win with all their soul.

Here in those realms of sweetness,
  'Mid blushing maidens fair,
Who cloth'd in grace and meekness
  With charms supremely rare.
They bow'd to take the prizes
  Which each had nobly won ;
Proud, when emotion rises,
  For deeds so bravely done.

Young Darlington had striven hard,
  Like Greeks in days of yore,
Charm'd with the wreaths of just reward
  Which triumphantly they bore,
While ringing cheers of honour
  Burst from the gather'd throng,
For swiftly-footed runner,
  Both hearty, loud, and long.

THE DARLINGTON LADIES' TRAINING COLLEGE CONVERSAZIONE,

HELD DECEMBER 10th, 1880.

The year was closing with its days
    When nights were long and drear,
Yet Luna cast her silver rays
    On friends that came to cheer.

Bright faces hail'd the guests with glee
    As through the hall they hied,
With charms and sweet serenity
    We hoped might aye abide.

There, fair ones bright with intellect
    Adorned that spacious hall,
With minds in studious thought bedeck'd,
    Sweet faces crowning all.

From distant homes these maidens came,
    And such they loved to prize,
Where sunny spots, with one grand aim
    They longed to realize.

Dear friends stood round whom they had made,
    Amid their studious hours;
Some few within that College shade,
    And some by sunny bowers.

And now that College work was done
   In which they'd laboured long,
They joyed o'er knowledge richly won,
   And laud it with a song.

Within that circle some were sad—
   Fill'd with an anxious care ;
Yet there were hearts both bright and glad,
   Ne'er yielding to despair.

The world was spread before their sight
   Like plains on some bright shore,
And hence life's battles they would fight
   Equipp'd with College lore.

Kind words were said and council given
   To those who soon would part,
The choicest words from under heaven
   To each young maiden's heart.

They sweetly sang their hymns of praise
   With Teachers watching by ;
The hymns they used each night to raise
   Like seraphs in the sky.

Farewells at last came from each one—
   For who should meet again—
Since College life for them was done,
   Which caused such mental strain.

O may they scatter rays of light
    Where'er their lot be cast,
And with their torch of knowledge bright
    Shine out o'er regions vast.

ADIEU TO DARLINGTON.

'Tis hard that I must say adieu
To friends who were both kind and true,
Whose tender hearts have ever been
With sweet affections, deep and keen.
Their mingled joys, their sorrows, too,
Made life, like flowers, tipp'd with the dew,
And what was more and sweeter still
My soul with holy joy would fill.
For in this world of change and care
They'd sweetly guide my life in prayer;
And must I say to hill and dell
A last adieu—a sad farewell—
To loving spots where I have been
O'er flowery beds and pastures green;—
By scenes where beech and hawthorn meet—
By streams that ripple at the feet—
By winding walks and shady bowers—
By villas deck'd with summer flowers—
By scenes where many a Sabbath bell
I've heard with music sweetly tell

Of gatherings to each holy pile
To worship there, in truth awhile?
O yes! there comes sad notes which say
I must from these soon pass away,
And leave for other ones to hear
Their notes upon the list'ning ear.
Yet, when I leave for other spheres
Their notes will sound upon my ears,
Then will I think of days no more,
And friends and scenes I loved before—
Of pleasures, when I mingled there
Under their sweet endearing care.
Then will my heart be fill'd with pain
That I no more will see again
Those scenes and friends of early days
And bask beneath their sunny rays.

SWEET AMBLESIDE.

Thou charming village of the vale,
   Where lofty mountains cleave the air,
Where beauty reigns within each dale;
   And all around is bright and fair;

Enraptured is the soul that views,
   From heights that in thy presence rise,
Those glowing scenes which Nature strews,
   Like visions through the vaulted skies.

Deep shadows paint the crested brow,
   Where mountains in their wildness stand,
Which vary all the picture through
   This graceful scene of mountain land.

The balmy heather scents the air,
   As west winds blow across each fell,
And every spot their fragrance share,
   Where round their heights such pleasures dwell.

The wild flowers find a shelter here,
   Where ferns profuse in wildness grow,
By streams that, ever fresh and clear,
   Down lofty hills and mountains flow.

The dashing spray from force and fall
   Unwearied is, with laughing song,
As day by day they cheerily call
   On those who at their fountains throng.

Here lovers sip the sparkling stream,
   And wish their lives might be as clear,
But O, how life seems like a dream,
   With mixed draughts so hard to cheer.

How oft, when cares men's life would sap,
   And weary toil would bear them down,
They've sheltered in thy rock-bound lap
   Till health hath placed on them its crown.

H

Within thy grasp, and by thy glades,
  The poets here have found a rest,
Where from thy bright and sunny shades,
  The world of thought have oft been blest.

How often at the eventide,
  When all is calm and sweet and fair,
The moon, like some entrancing bride,
  Would o'er the lake her beauties share.

Till every rippling wave would shine
  With such a dazzling glare of gold,
That fancy bursts the fairy mine
  Where thought her untold treasures hold.

I love thy soft and silver streams,
  I love thy mossy-shaded glens,
I love thy lake when sunlit beams
  O'er all its placid bosom bends.

Then let me here oft find a day
  To ramble o'er, by mount and hill,
And to th' Eternal, homage pay,
  For all the workings of His will.

ON THE LATE SIR HENRY HAVELOCK, C.B., K.C.B.

General Sir Henry Havelock, the Christian soldier, was born at Ford Hall, Bishopwearmouth, in 1795, and died in 1857, just six days after the relief of Lucknow. He was 40 years in the service, 32 of which he spent in India. Six times his horse was shot under him, and once he was shipwrecked. He went through the Afghanistan War, he was at the storming of Ghuznee, and at the forcing of the famous Cabool Pass; had many engagements with the Sepoys at Cawnpore. Shut up in Lucknow with his half-starved troops, he defended the women and children until relieved by his brother veteran, Sir Colin Campbell (afterwards Lord Clyde). Some years ago, the author was informed, Mr. R. H. Allan, J.P., of Blackwell Hall, his near relative, intended the Grange Hall, Darlington, as a residence for him, had he been spared to return to England. It is gratifying to know that his gallant son, the M.P. for Sunderland, has settled down on the Banks of the Tees at Blackwell.

How oft the muse with fervid fire
Hath wakened up the poet's lyre,
To sing of men who bravely bore
Their countries' flag through fields of gore;
To free their sons from chains that bound
Their victims to a tyrant's ground.
The gallant sons of ancient Gaul,
With might and power obeyed the call,
With those who by a noble will,
Moved armies with a warrior's skill.
Old Rome, whose chieftains often led
Their legions where brave soldiers bled;
And Spartans, too, who dared to die,
And all their deadly foes defy.

Shall we not then in history's scroll
Record the men of patriot soul,
Their deeds extol and laud their name
To ages of undying fame?
    No bolder, braver, ever led
Their gallant hosts, where tyrants fled
By sea or land, on hill or vale,
Their foes they boldly would assail.
They ne'er would stoop, nor would they bend,
For Britons will the right defend,
Like heroes true and warriors brave
On battle field or crested wave,
Their country's flag by might and main
Though great their odds, they will sustain.
    Now foremost in the foremost ranks
Brave Havelock all the brave outflanks;
For never once upon the field
Would he his country's prestige yield,
But true in soul and brave in heart
From truth and right he ne'er would part.
He, on to victory armies led,
And foes before him rashly fled,
Till by his power and master skill
They bowed submissive to his will.
    Had he been spared our walks to range,
And dwell in peace at " Allan's Grange,"
That ancient seat which nobly stands
Amid our richest pasture lands,

Where stately trees and lovely flowers
Beguile the heart in sunny hours;
Where all is fair round that domain,
With views that reach the German main.
How we had welcomed his return,
While our proud hearts within would burn,
Had Providence designed it so
E're he should sleep in dust below.
But He who watched him thought it best
To let the warrior longer rest,
That after many a weary fight
On India's plains, the gallant knight
Should claim a crown, more lasting far
Than laurel crown, or soldier's star;
So like the brave he calmly sleeps
Where no strict guard, the watch-tower keeps,
And not with us, 'mid sylvan shades,
Close by the Tees, when evening fades.
    Long may his son, who shared his toils
Amid the storm of Indian broils,
Where Nana Sahib's trait'rous guile
Caused British blood to flow the while,
May he be spared, long years to share
The laurels which the victor's wear;
And live in honour and renown,
Of him, who too should shar'd the crown.
Now English hearts can ne'er forget
The trials which those soldiers met,

On India's burning sand and plain,
Where noble ones o'erpowered, were slain.
To such, our country owns its fame,
More highly than an Emperor's name;
All honour then to sire and son
For all the victories they have won,
And as we pass that ancient hall
We'll often to our minds recall
Those heroes of undying fame
And lofty Havelock's honoured name.

THE POET'S PET CAT.

I have a cat, 'tis white and grey,
'Tis full of frolic, full of play ;
It gives its owner much delight,
In early morn or dewy night;
It thrumbs and plays when I am near,
Thus many an hour it gives me cheer.
It trips along with velvet feet,
And seems so glad when mine they meet;
When near the house my steps it hears,
It lifts its head and cocks its ears,
Then bounds along, both swift and sure,
To meet me at the passage door.
One little life I always find
To me is true, to me is kind,;

Sometimes the world, with shrivell'd soul,
May give a smile—next give a scowl,
Though reason it may claim to share,
Yet narrow-minded hearts are there,
And cold and stiff the hand is found,
With colder looks and growling sound;
But pussy's instinct feels no cold,
'Tis warm and true—'tis pleased and bold.
Its eyes are bright when night is dark;
Its paws are soft, they leave no mark;
And cold indeed that heart must be
That cannot see a joy in thee.
My books it seems to know and prize,
And watches with its sparkling eyes;
And when I write 'tis just the same,
And knows right well its favoured name.
Despise not, then, my little pet,
Nor murmur out one sad regret;
For if the world is false and hard,
And treats you with a cold regard,
There is one little life that's true,
And oh! poor pussy, that is you.

THE GOLDEN AGE.

Had fortune with her golden wand,
　　Designed that I its wreath should wear;
How vast the throng my friends would be,
　　Her tinseled flowers with me to share.

The golden gates of Prince and Lord
　　Would open with a ready hand,
'Mid gorgeous halls my feet would tread
　　In visions of a fairy land.

And Crœsus in his state and power
　　Would seat me by his golden throne;
Where minions lowly bend and bow
　　Their sins of mammon to atone.

Miss Kilminseg with golden leg
　　Would stump the Hall a golden Queen;
While Lords of golden lace would pace
　　With pageant shew the glittering scene.

Could brains for once be ushered in
　　Without a golden badge or star;
The Gods would thunder out aloud,
　　" Now let the gates stand out ajar,"

This is the spot where Cæsar reigns,
　　Why let such clods as Virgil in;
Gold, gold, not educated brains,
　　They are so poor and soft and thin.

The golden crown and dazzling star
   That dangles on the minion's breast;
Outweighs a Homer's head by far
   Or all his lofty soul possess'd.

But, O, to share one beaming thought,
   From that ennobled lofty mind,
And in our own be firmly wrought,
   'Twould be a prize, gold could not find.

Then let me live with men adorned,
   With riches of a stirling worth;
The wealth which toiling minds have earned,
   From studious thought and not from birth.

GOD'S GIFT OF FLOWERS.

What gems of love God kindly gives
   To all His creatures here,
To beautify the plains of earth,
   And give His creatures cheer.

Sweet flowers He sends with rich perfume,
   In colours bright and gay,
With sunlit beams and golden clouds,
   To help us on our way.

The Violet with its modest head
  Concealed beneath the leaves,
The scented Rose in sweetness fair
  Which no heart e'er deceives.

And Ferns that in their wildness grow,
  By heath or mountain side,
They cheer us with their spiral wings
  Like smiles that grace a bride.

Beneath the shade of some lone grove,
  Or by the rippling stream,
They lift their shining leafy heads
  Like angels, in a dream.

Then thanks to Him who gave us those
  Sweet flowers to love and prize,
They soften down the cares of life,
  And joys through them arise.

ANNIVERSARY HYMN.
ON JUDAH'S FERTILE PLAIN.

Set to Music by Mr. J. Hoggett.

On Judah's fertile plain
  The peaceful shepherds lay,
No ill their flocks sustain,
  They wait the break of day;
But heavenly music soft and sweet
Their ears in wondrous accents greet.

For lo ! in Bethlehem
   The Prince of Peace is born ;
No earthly diadem
   Doth his fair brow adorn :
But He shall sway His sceptre wide,
And Kings shall in His love confide.

Our native land hath caught
   The music of His name,
By teachers who have taught
   His loving power and fame.
And we will sing of Jesus too
Whose name is sweet as morning dew.

And we will sing the more
   That truth the angels told,
Who from yon shining shore
   Sang in the shepherds' fold,
Till all the world that King adore
Who lives and reigns for evermore.

Let children everywhere
   Their sweetest praises sing,
And all His favour share,
   The blessings of their King,
That when these choirs on earth shall cease,
They'll sing upon the plains of peace.

ON THE PARADISE CHAPEL LADIES'
SEWING MEETING.

O for some cunning elf to guide my thoughtful pen,
To steer it clear of self, and from young thoughtless men.
Here in this busy place, where pliant hands are found,
The smile of woman's face lights up the circle round.
The lays of ancient Rome, might claim a poet's fame,
And visions of sweet home, immortalize a name,
But here in Paradise, 'mid gay ones bright and fair,
E'en fields of frozen ice, would melt with hearts so rare ;
With sympathies so pure, on labour so intent,
Would make a poet sure, on goodness all were bent,
The steady needle eye, the sewing-stitch machine,
Seem through the webs to fly where work is done so clean.
Each leaves her fireside, where comforts richly reign,
To cut and stitch with pride the fancy and the plain,
The smart-shaped amber frock, embroidered and so neat,
The well-knit worsted sock, to fit on any feet.
The Pastor's wife goes round, and chuckles all the while,
Ties on a badge profound, then leaves you with a smile,
Another follows quick, to bid you welcome here,
And when you have to "tip" they all send forth a cheer;
They say 'tis for the cause, you must not then rebel,
Or else, by woman's laws, they soon will you expel.
Then Florence comes, so neat, with *olive flask* in hand,
And O, her smiles so sweet, no soul can long
    withstand.

The married ladies ply their needles quick and well,
They give a glance so sly, yet never break the spell.
Thus hour by hour glides by, till Congou comes in sight,
When greetings all run high, and everything goes right.
This hive is full of bees, with honey-moons in store,
And if you taste their teas, your lips will long for more.
They flutter on the wing, if they dont with their heart,
Such creatures never sting, though oft they make you
 smart.
They fly from flower to flower, as only bees can do,
They buzz about each bow'r, and on them sweetness
 strew ;
One Queen Bee is Miss Gledding, who smiles so like
 a bride,
Yet keeps from every wedding, whatever joys betide.
The other is Miss Kipling, who veto's every chance
Of Parson, Peer, or stripling, and breaks o'er them
 her lance.
There are others of renown, and other gentle folks—
The plodding sisters Brown and happy sister Stokes.
Now if this train of thought be call'd a sad digression,
The Elf will soon be brought before a *Brewis*ter session
Some penance to atone, with shoes well filled with peas,
As far as Bulmer's Stone, upon his bended knees,
Hence to the Super's care, or else to Scott himself—
They'll cage him like a bear, this wicked little Elf.
The frenzied eye can see both young heads and the old,
So Elfin's pen must be a pen of sterling gold.

To sketch each charming face, and do it too with ease,
To give it taste and grace, the critic's eye to please.
Now time would fail to tell of those who mingle here,
Who work so hard and well, and do it with a cheer.
How pleasant then to spend an hour in such a court,
Yet all things have an end, and this one seems *too short*.

ON THE LIBERAL GATHERING IN THE CENTRAL HALL,

On Saturday Night, April 3rd, 1880.

The sturdy Liberals of the South
   Were gathered in the spacious Hall,
To greet the champions of the truth,
   And triumph o'er the foeman's fall.

The fairest flowers of southern climes
   Bedeck'd the room in colours fair,
Sweet emblems of more happy times
   When Britons shall her bounties share.

Around the walls bright banners hung,
   Fair trophies of proud victories gain'd
While cheers from valiant leaders rung,
   In honour of the work sustained.

Young Lambton stripp'd his soldier's sword
   To battle for a nobler cause,
To struggle with his soul and word
   For his and for his country's laws.

And Pease, the tried and favourite choice
    Of Durham, and the Liberal race,
Who, with his clear out-spoken voice,
    Has gain'd for him his honoured place.

These men, with hearts both true and brave,
    Will triumph in the coming strife,
And soon the laurel branch will wave
    With honours o'er their future life.

And Arthur, too, the Whitby pet,
    Who wore with pride his laurel crown,
Beset in fairest Whitby jet,
    Shall live in honour and renown.

And Fry, who with a modest mien,
    Paced through the file of Liberal ranks,
With his beloved spouse and queen,
    To tender his unfeigned thanks.

Thus through the Hall 'mid music's strains,
    The conquerors and the conquering came:
To glory in the brilliant gains,
    And cheer with pride the victor's name.

Each led and marshall'd by a mind
    Which, in some future day, shall be
A guiding star to humankind
    In counsels of their destiny.

Yes, Dale shall be the people's choice,
   In some fair Liberal city near,
When Liberal hearts will all rejoice
   To welcome one without a peer.

Brave Britons shall their banners wave
   O'er peoples near and countries far—
For they detest the name of slave,
   Who love sweet peace and loathe sad war.

CORPORATION SUNDAY, DARLINGTON,

When T. R. M. Plews, Esq., The Mayor ; Hugh Dunn, Esq., Town Clerk ; The Aldermen, Town Councillors and others, walked in procession to St. Cuthbert's Parish Church, on Sunday, Nov. 26th, 1876. The Rev. T. E. Hodgson, preached a Sermon on behalf of the Hospital.

'Twas Autumn, when the leaves were sear,
The foggiest season of the year,
When invitations, trim and bright,
Were given, to the town's delight.
'Twas from a sire who claimed to be
The Bench's highest dignity ;
Who, with a generous heart and will,
Inclined to keep the custom still—
Of ancient date and wide renown,
Where once a year they walked the town.
The guests assembled at the Hall
Who thus obeyed that magnate's call ;

And, once refreshed with what was there,
Thence to St. Cuthbert's did repair.
Now, first who took the early start
Was one who, dressed in gold so smart,
Strode on with an Imperial air,
As if he was in fact the Mayor.
Then came the Clerk, with curly wig;
Calm as a Judge—yet not so big—
Whose face was truly grave, yet gay
As through the crowd he marched his way.
Next came the Mayor with golden chain,
Designed o'er us a year to reign,
But woe to those whom he may chain,
They'll not like him to see again.
Then Aldermen and Councillors too—
The men who have the work to do,
Marched by in solemn rank and file,
So grave as if they ne'er could smile;
Nor in their councils break a lance,
When needful works some would advance,
Whether of gas or of the Skerne,
They many a wounded heart have borne.
Then came in style, both clean and neat,
Who round our homes keep up the beat—
The men who both by night and day
On watch-towers keep the foe away.
Next came in step the Rifle Corps,

In marching time, as if before
The Queen, who all of them adore;
While led by music's softest strains,
Their destined end in silence gains.
The faithful Priest, in surplice white,
His worthy hearers now invite
To join with him in solemn prayer.
The service which had brought them there.
'Twas in his heart to give advice,
In sober words, of costly price,
That those who had much gold in store
Might give a balm to heal the sore,
And comfort those who, sick and poor,
Were longing for a speedy cure;
To those who ill and wounded lay,
The waking night and restless day;
And he who gave was well repaid,
In giving to the sick their aid.
Such recompense will surely find
The sympathies of human kind;
And in that great and final day
A high reward the Judge will pay.

REMINISCENCES OF THE PAST.

Yes, one by one, men pass away
   From life's beclouded station,
No power for long can it delay
   In any clime or nation;
The monarch on his gilded throne
   May try Time's hand to muffle,
But he will find a power alone
   His mortal coil to shuffle.

The man who steered the ship of state
   O'er rock-bound seas of trouble,
Hath found his strength with Time's rude fate
   Burn up his power like stubble.
Proud nations cringed at his command
   When he sent forth his dictum,
Yet stood aghast at Death's thin hand,
   And fell, alas, its victim.

The loving heart that beat so free
   Within a Royal sister,
A nation's wail for her shall be—
   For all, alas, have missed her;
The good alone will ever find
   A sympathising nation,
Its people's heart to always bind,
   However wide the station.

The laurel wreath that deck'd the brave
  Of a soldier for his daring,
Shall lie a covering o'er his grave
  While Death his star is wearing.
On battle fields, amid the slain,
  He sought and fought for glory,
But meets a foe, whose deadly reign
  Slays young heads and the hoary.

Time's hand hath dealt the fatal blow
  In many a house so humble.
But true ones knew God will'd it so,
  And would not therefore grumble.
The velvet hand of Time will be
  A solace to the weary,
And point like stars where moments flee
  Through paths that's dark and dreary.

Though Time roll's on with rapid pace
  And cuts off those we cherished,
And hides from us the form and face
  Of those in life we nourished.
But visions of sweet hope come nigh,
  The saddened soul to brighten
Which turns to joy the heart's deep sigh,
  And burden'd ones to lighten.

Are not the deeds of nations dead,
  Still upward, onward moving?

Are not the thoughts which we have read
Of men and lives so loving
Impelling all to work and try
To make earth's burdens lighter,
That when Time calls for us to die
We'll leave it all the brighter?

THE MOUNTAIN DAISY.

Music by Mr. J. Hoggett.

There is a mountain daisy,
The sweetest of its kind,
It looks so rich and racy,
The like I ne'er could find.
The flowers that grow beside it
Look fresh and fair, 'tis true;
But that one little daisy
Is like the sparkling dew.

When Phœbus shines upon it,
'Tis like the morning star.
I fain would try to con it,
If I but only dare.
It is upon the mountain
Almost beyond my reach,
And I'm afraid of counting
The lessons it might teach.

If I should reach and miss it,
  My life a plague would be.
I want to love and kiss it
  That it may sweeter be.
I'd leave all other flowers
  For other hands to cull,
Could I among the bowers
  This little daisy pull.

The blue bell is as smiling,
  Forget-me-not's are fair,
And other flowers beguiling,
  Grow round in sweetness there.
But the daisy on the mountain
  With golden cap is crowned,
Like rays that gild the fountain
  Where sparkling drops are found.

Clear streams around may wander
  Where other flow'rets grow,
With colours gay and grandeur,
  But these are all a show.
My daisy is the sweetest,
  That crowns the mountain crest,
I vow it is the neatest,
  And sure will suit me best.

GERTIE.

A little maiden, thin and spare,
 Lay on a bed of oaten straw,
Her face was pale, her covering bare,
 And at her heart a worm did gnaw.

Her room was in a lonely lane,
 The sun scarce ever shone therein,
But winds blew through a broken pane,
 Over a form both wan and thin.

She listened to the children's play,
 And heard the sweet birds often sing,
For it was now the month of May,
 The joyous days of flowery spring.

Her little heart was beating fast,
 To think how gladsome all appeared,
Though every earthly hope seem'd past,
 As to the future world she neared.

Did no one care for her within?
 Was she forgot as crowds pass'd by?
Could she no love or pity win?
 Did no one stop to hear her sigh?

It chanced a schoolboy on his way
 Look'd in, as schoolboys often do,
And there a sickly maiden lay,
 Poor and pale, with comforts few.

The orange which his mother gave
　　That morn he pass'd it through the pane,
He wished that maiden's life to save,
　　And give her health like his again.

And other schoolboys on their way
　　Would give, as this brave boy had given;
While she her hand would raise and say,
　　" Thank God and you, for gifts of heaven."

One morn he came with flowers to give;
　　No hand was there to take them in.
He wondered—" Does the maiden live;
　　Where is that hand so wan and thin? "

He looked, but grief soon filled his heart,
　　For there he saw the shroud and bier
Of her who shared with him a part
　　The fruit and flowers he left to cheer.

And so he stood with sighs and tears,
　　While others gathered round him too.
They asked—Why thus his grief and fears?
　　Why does he make so much to do?

He plainly told them why he sighed,
　　For he had feelings for the poor;
And wept because the girl had died,
　　And he would help that hand no more.

And then he told his little mates
   That Gertie now was really dead ;
That she had passed the golden gates,
   And left her poor and lonely shed.

Then came the thought that they had done
   One generous act to lessen woe ;
And their young hearts a peace had won,
   Which gems or gold could ne'er bestow.

THE SETTING OF THE SUN IN[N] DARLINGTON.

I've stood upon the moss-clad hill,
   And watched the Sun, in summer set ;
I've seen his rays the valleys fill
   With splendour I can ne'er forget,
His golden wings tip'd every tree,
   His light flashed out on every flower,
And hill and vale appeared to be
   Illumined with the golden shower.
And then I've seen the thick dark cloud
   In tempests gather round his shield,
As if the gods would throw a shroud,
   Over some gory battle-field ;
But then I've seen it pass away,
   And stars peer out on every side,
When that great light of joyful day
   Had gone to other lands, a guide.

I've stood upon another hill,
   And often watched another *Sun*,
A *Sun* whose rays with death would fill
   That darksome vale where he had run.
No genial warmth from it was felt,
   No golden streams from it did flow;
Its highest heat could never melt
   The frozen hearts of sin and woe,
But every ray was known to yield
   A deadly pang to all who basked
Beneath its dark distrustful shield,
   Or madly for its favours asked;
But it has set—for ever set,
   Its gloomy rays for ever gone,
Nor can its victims e'er forget
   The thousand ills which it has done.
O that a thousand *Moons* and *Stars*,
   Like that base light, would now depart,
The earth would shine out brighter far,
   And cheer up many a gloomy heart.

FOR AN AUTOGRAPH ALBUM.

How oft a *name* brings forth to mind
   The long forgotten thought of those,
Who in some darksome hour we find
   Have gone to take a long repose.

In early days when they were young,
  And life's pulsation beat full high ;
How many a noble thought was wrung,
  To lead their spirits to the sky.

But Time's rude hand unceasing pushed
  Life's fragil craft along the stream ;
And gone, like some fair rose that blushed
  Or like the vision of a dream.

And he who writes may leave a *name*,
  Which some in distant years may see,
O may it sweet emotions claim,
  From hearts where love of Christ shall be.

ON THE CENTENARY GATHERING OF DISSENTING SUNDAY SCHOOLS IN DARLINGTON,

AUGUST 3rd, 1880.

'Twas sweet to see the gathering hosts
  Of scholars blithe and gay,
With cheerful hearts and gladsome souls,
  To Raikes a tribute pay.

The happy day they longed to see
  Came with an azure sky,
And O ! the joy that filled each soul
  Was seen by every eye.

With lightsome step and cheerful face
  They bounded o'er the ground;
No lagging foot on all the way
  Could in each rank be found.

They marched to music's mellow sound,
  Like soldiers to review;
But they were soldiers of the Cross,
  With laurel leaves to strew.

Bright banners floated on the breeze,
  With many a sweet device—
" The Sabbath School," " The Shepherd's Fold,"
  " The Cross—its costly price."

And so they sang their sabbath song,
  With teachers by their side,
And silver sounds from young ones rose
  Where schools for honour vied.

'Twas sweet to see old scholars near,
  Who in those schools had been;
They blessed the children as they pass'd
  The grouping ranks between.

A tear would glisten in the eye,
  Touched by some tender chord,
When they remembered in their youth
  They read God's precious word.

This day six thousand youthful souls
 Will prize life's journey through;
For smiles from Heaven came sweetly down
 Like sunbeams on the dew.

Could Raikes the founder but have seen
 This Christian work of love;
His entranced soul with praise would sing
 In his bright home above.

TO THE REV. FRANCIS MARRS ON HIS MARR-AGE.

AUGUST, 1879.

Once on a time the mighty Mars
Began a tour among the stars,
And silent through ethereal space
He lifted high his ruddy face.
He, light-hearted, wandered on
Through regions few had ever gone,
Past constellations fair and bright
He onward roved both day and night,
Admiring much their varied form,
In Summer's shade and Winter's storm.
The secret was, he sought somehow,
As through wide space his honour flew,
That he a satellite might win,
And so another life begin,

For bulky orbs both bright and fair
Had even got a shining pair.
No wonder then his ruddy hue
In deeper shades of colour grew.
For lo ! he wandered long and late
Without a fair and shining mate.
And thus among the distant spheres
He sought for one with anxious fears.
No comet's glance would he e'er take—
No transient bargain ever make ;
On Mars, they never could prevail
To woo a maid so precious pale. .
Who lived somewhat a roving life—
Now fancy her to make a wife,
Such maidens thus might coy the tars,.
But never so with ruddy Mars.
Nor meteors, who would lift their heads,
Then laugh to scorn the star she weds.
No, no ! this planet plann'd his work,
And so his schemes they ne'er could burk.
He eyed fair Venus, sweet and bright,
Shining forth with her dazzling light,
But thought she look'd too gorgeous far
To be a mate for such a star ;
And so he bent his onward way
To gain some form, less proud and gay ;
And by the signs, the ancients told
He braced his mind in visions bold,

Then glanced at all the fairy throng
And said, " Why sure this can't be wrong,"
For with a gladsome heart he found .
A satellite both safe and sound. .
He kept in view one star, so bright,
In high noonday and darksome night,
Till by attraction's laws, he tried
To gravitate it for his bride.
On other orbs the belt he traced,
As through the Zodiac lines they paced,
And here he found strange figures trooped
In various ways, by ancients grouped.
He passed by Twins, and Balances, and Rams,
And Crabs and Scorpions, if not Lambs,
At least a Lion, Goat, and Bull,
And Waterman with pitcher full :
An Archer, with his bow full bent,
And Fishes, fit for days in Lent,
But, as he passed his friend Leo,
He spied a form called sweet Virgo ;
He paused at such a lovely sight,
And said, " I'll have this satellite."
And so, from regions bright as day,
He brought her from the milky way.
Thence to the Northern hemisphere
He took his little precious dear.
And, as the moon was near its full,
He took her to the shores of Mull ;

For sure on pleasure he was bent,
And to Oban he forward went.
His honeymoon began to wane,
And so he thought of home again,
And thus in Paradise to-day
He brought her all the weary way,
And promised true his star to shield,
E'en in the regions of Nestfield ;
And those who gaze on stars are led
To say, " that Mars has wisely wed."

ON REV. J. G. PEARSON, LATE VICAR OF DARLINGTON,

WHO DIED JUNE 20th, 1873, AGED 61 YEARS.

He hath gone to the grave. and passed to his rest,
Where the robed ones of light for ever are blest—
Where prophets and martyrs and angels survey
The glories that gleam on that pearl-paved way.

Where the Saviour, enthroned in beauty and grace,
Sheds a lustre supreme on each loving face ;
And the sorrow and pain which each felt below,
Are forgot when they look on His star-spangled brow.

The people may mourn that their pastor's no more,
And with sorrow his loss they all may deplore,
When they think how he taught them of heavenly things,
And lured them above, as on cherubic wings.

How he joined them in praise, and soothed them in
    prayer,
Till they felt in their hearts it was good to be there ;
How the widow rejoiced, when he knelt by her side
Till by faith she beheld the Great Crucified.

Then her soul, like the calm of an unruffled lake,
Felt a sweet peace within, the world cannot take—
Which the rarest of rubies never can buy,
Because it comes forth from God's Spirit on high.

A cloud might betimes overshadow his life,
As he struggled along amid earth's busy strife ;
Yet pilgrim-like, his lone path he pursued,
Till the sun shone again, dispersing the cloud.

No more in God's House will his voice e'er be heard,
To gladden the heart with his comforting word ;
But on high, from the throne, in echoes will sound—
" Come follow the Lord 'till with Him you are found."

FOUNTAIN'S ABBEY, STUDLEY ROYAL.

    Awake ! thou muse, in pleasing strains,
        Help me in tune to string my lyre—
    To sing of Studley's vast domains,
        Of holy monk and burly friar.

    In days of yore, 'mid sylvan groves
        The sportsman followed up the deer,
    When wandering in unnumbered droves,
        Where glide these silver streams so clear.

J

The monk would leave his lonely cell,
   The knight his love a time forsake,
To rove o'er mossy hill and dell,
   Where hunters' horns the vales awake.

Here, in those scenes of nature's power,
   Like Eden, with its pastures green,
Fair Fountain rears its stately tower,
   With many a noble oak between.

Within its walks the ancient yew
   Still stands, where many a knight has bent
To take a last and sad adieu,
   Ere he to deadly conflicts went.

The blazing fire has often here
   The merry monk with joy inspired,
As he beheld in Christmas cheer
   The dainty dish his heart admired.

Now, in these shades, 'mid crumbling dust,
   The abbot and his friars lie,
Who once with kingly state and trust
   Could even kingly powers defy.

And in those walls, where kings and queens
   Have sung their matins clear and sweet,
Defiant Time hath changed the scenes,
   For owls to find a safe retreat.

'Tis strange, when o'er these spots you tread,
　　To muse on monkish times and rites—
To think the life those abbots led,
　　Far from a world's entranc'd delights.

Where Robin, famed in history's page,
　　Contested with the friar's might,
Till he no more the war would wage,
　　And deemed the friar in the right.

How changed is every spot around
　　Since these recluses reigned in power,
Or knelt upon the sacred ground
　　In the silent midnight hour !

The sacred altars, where are they ?
　　Or holy priests, who incense burnt ?
To dark oblivion pass'd away—
　　Their souls have now the secret learnt.

How changed the groves where stately trees,
　　In all their native grandeur grew ;
Where quivered in the autumn breeze,
　　The kingly oak, the sacred yew.

Still, in these fairy lands some rise
　　Where cultured minds have shap'd the sites,
Where classic beauties please the eyes,
　　Amid those haunts of monkish rites.

The Abbey, though in ruins, stands
  Glorious in this sheltered dale ;
Is kept from rude and ruthless hands—
  A nation's pride, a history's tale.

Long may the noble Marquis live
  Who owns those classic scenes so fair,
Which to admiring spirits give
  Entrancing pleasures, rich and rare.   .

This wondrous pile of Early English architecture was
founded by John of York, the first abbot, in the 12th century.
It is considered one of the most beautiful in England, and
though Time has laid his withering hand upon some of its
parts, enough is left to give the tourist and antiquarian an
accurate idea of its beauty and extent.   One of the many yew
trees is still left growing, said to be 800 years old.   Nineteen
of its abbots lie interred within the walls.   The Abbey was, in
1540, sold, and many of its buildings pulled down to furnish the
proprietor with material to build his mansion.

ON THE HOAR FROST

OF JANUARY 25TH, 1881.

How vast the source fair nature yields
  To man's enquiring mind,
'Mid starry worlds or flowery fields
  What pleasures he can find.

When verdant Spring comes laughing in
  To cheer him on his way ;
When early flowers his praises win
  As bright birds round them play.

When Summer comes with garlands fair
   And fruit to tempt his eye;
When balmy breezes fill the air
   With scarce a muttered sigh.

When Autumn sun-sets gild the sky
   With golden rays of right,
As fleecy clouds are passing by
   With silver linings bright.

Men often wish they'd always be
   Who dread the Winter's blast;
As if they could no beauties see
   To charm when those are past.

Yet Winter comes to change the view
   With snow so pure and white;
With crystal grains of morning dew,
   Both beautiful and bright.

The frozen stream, the bracing breeze,
   Comes with a welcome charm,
For youth to sport where rivers freeze
   And make their heart's blood warm.

But when they see the bright hoar frost
   On trees that round them stand,
With admiration they are lost
   In such a fairy land.

'Tis as if the Eternal One
   Had opened up to sight
The pearl-decked plain, where fountains run,
   Throughout the realms of light.

When Heaven's pure bliss pervaded all
   The glories of the seen,
And man had risen from his fall
   And stood where God had been.

It seemed as if for one short day
   Earth had been purged of sin,—
That Heaven had lifted up its veil
   And let the glory in.

The hallowed yew's outspreading bows
   Was cased with silver spray,
And with its shene, a glory throws
   Around each sparkling ray.

The graceful fir, with stately mien
   Stood peering to the sky,
With diamond drops, like some fair Queen
   With noble courtiers by.

The Holly's leaf was silver fringed,
   The Beech was crystalized
The Oak with sun-lit stars was tinged
   And Heaven was realised.

If Winter comes then with its ills
It comes with glory too,
With transformed shrubs and snow-draped hills
To man's enraptured view.

OUR YOUNG MEN.

DEDICATED TO THE MEMBERS OF THE YOUNG MEN'S CHRISTIAN ASSOCIATION, DARLINGTON.

The world needs light, clear Christian light,
But who the torch will bear?
The good lies shrouded in the night
Of sin and dark despair.
The young that torch will proudly bear,
Though fiends in hosts stand by;
They'll lift it in the high mid air,
And all their powers defy.

Poor drunkards, who are lost in vice,
Who heed no Sabbath bell;
But, led by Satan's dark devise,
Their souls in darkness dwell.
Their earthly homes no comforts know,
They're demons in disguise;
But these young Christian friends will show
The path where virtue lies.

Poor erring youth, who think the earth
Is full of golden dreams,
Where temples sound with songs of mirth,
And all with pleasure gleams.

But they forget, as thus they think,
   The cup is filled with woe ;
And bound by custom's fettering link
   They on in madness go.

Our Lord, with His great loving heart—
   Supplied with heavenly food—
Was ever ready to impart,
   And do His creatures good.
From early dawn to weary night,
   By city, stream, and lake,
He went dispensing truths and light
   For His dear children's sake.

Go, then, and join that Christian band—
   The world needs all your aid—
To scatter seeds through all the land,
   And you will be repaid.
The climes of light where Jesus reigns
   Will be your sure reward,
To range the amaranthine plains
   With nothing to retard.

Wm. Stairmand, Printer, 1, Horse Market, Darlington.